ARIZONA NIGHTS

BY

STEWART EDWARD WHITE

Illustrations by N. C. Wyeth

The Rio Grande Press, Inc.

GLORIETA, NEW MEXICO · 87535

First TRGP Printing 1985

A Rio Grande Classic
First Published in 1907

L.C. Card Catalog 85-62267

ISBN No.: 0-87380-155-5

The Rio Grande Press, Inc.
GLORIETA, NEW MEXICO · 87535

PUBLISHER'S PREFACE

Stewart Edward White (1873-1946) wrote this fine book based on his own personal experiences. The story-telling idiom is of his time and milieu. Riding the range as a cowpoke in those days was precisely the way he describes it, eighty years ago. *Arizona Nights* has become a classic of its genre.

We have copied this edition from a copy of the book published in 1907—the first edition—by Grosset & Dunlap of New York. Our printing experts tell us the original type was probably handset letter by letter, and hence, subject to typesetting errors. This first edition was printed on soft sulfite (wood pulp) paper, which in those days yielded often-imperfect printing—as in this book. Thus, our facsimile edition (slightly enlarged) shows in a few places some of the same, incorrectible faults printed in the first edition. We regret that, but the result is, nevertheless, a faithful replica of a first edition except for these words here.

Artist Newell Convers Wyeth, father of the contemporary artist Andrew Newell Wyeth, illustrated the first edition of this title with four paintings. They were not well printed in 1907, but we have had them reproduced here with computer techniques and we believe they appear better in our edition than in the first edition.

Our good friend on the faculty of the University of Arizona, Dr. Bernard (Bunny) L. Fontana, Ph.D., recommended this book as a fiction classic of the Southwest, and urged us to reprint it. We found it altogether delightful reading, comparable in style and context to our highly popular *Black Range Tales,* by James A. McKenna. It was also highly recommended by friend David Laird, Librarian at the U. of A. Library. Both gentlemen are experts in Southwestern Americana, as well as good friends of ours.

This is the first fiction/fact title the Rio Grande Press has published—all preceding books (125 of them) have been authentic historical materials generally written at the time written about, i.e., first person adventures. The story line here may be fiction, but the range-riding cow-poking background is as authentic as the Arizona desert.

Robert B. McCoy

La Casa Escuela
Glorieta, N.M. 87535
September 1985

Called him out and shot him in the stomach

ARIZONA NIGHTS

BY

STEWART EDWARD WHITE

Illustrations by N. C. Wyeth

GROSSET & DUNLAP

PUBLISHERS   NEW YORK

CONTENTS

PART I

ARIZONA NIGHTS

PART II

THE TWO-GUN MAN

CONTENTS

PART I

ARIZONA NIGHTS

CHAPTER ONE

THE OLE VIRGINIA

THE ring around the sun had thickened all day long, and the turquoise blue of the Arizona sky had filmed. Storms in the dry countries are infrequent, but heavy; and this surely meant storm. We had ridden since sun-up over broad mesas, down and out of deep cañons, along the base of the mountains in the wildest parts of the territory. The cattle were winding leisurely toward the high country; the jack rabbits had disappeared; the quail lacked; we did not see a single antelope in the open.

"It's a case of hole up," the Cattleman ventured his opinion. "I have a ranch over in the Double R. Charley and Windy Bill hold it down. We'll tackle it. What do you think?"

The four cowboys agreed. We dropped into a low, broad watercourse, ascended its bed to big cottonwoods and flowing water, followed it into box cañons between rim-rock carved fantastically and painted like a Moorish façade, until at last in a widening below a rounded hill, we came upon an adobe house, a fruit tree, and a round corral. This was the Double R.

Charley and Windy Bill welcomed us with soda biscuits. We turned our horses out, spread our beds on the floor, filled our pipes, and squatted on our heels. Various dogs of various breeds investigated us. It was very pleasant, and we did not mind the ring around the sun.

"Somebody else coming," announced the Cattleman finally.

"Uncle Jim," said Charley, after a glance.

A hawk-faced old man with a long white beard and long white hair rode out from the cottonwoods. He had on a battered broad hat abnormally high of crown, carried across his saddle a heavy "eight square" rifle, and was followed by a half-dozen lolloping hounds.

The largest and fiercest of the latter, catching sight of our group, launched himself with lightning rapidity at the biggest of the ranch dogs, promptly nailed that canine by the back of the neck, shook him violently a score of times, flung him aside, and pounced on the next. During the ensuing few moments that hound was the busiest thing in the West. He satisfactorily whipped four dogs, pursued two cats up a tree, upset the Dutch oven and the rest of the soda biscuits, stampeded the horses, and raised a cloud of dust adequate to represent the smoke of battle. We others were too paralysed to move. Uncle Jim sat placidly on his white horse, his thin knees bent to the ox-bow stirrups, smoking.

In ten seconds the trouble was over, principally because there was no more trouble to make. The hound returned leisurely, licking from his chops the hair of his victims. Uncle Jim shook his head.

" Trailer," said he sadly, " is a little severe."

We agreed heartily, and turned in to welcome Uncle Jim with a fresh batch of soda biscuits.

The old man was one of the typical " long hairs." He had come to the Galiuro Mountains in '69, and since '69 he had remained in the Galiuro Mountains, spite of man or the devil. At present he possessed some hundreds of cattle, which he was reputed to water, in a dry season, from an ordinary dishpan. In times past he had prospected.

That evening, the severe Trailer having dropped

to slumber, he held forth on big-game hunting and dogs, quartz claims and Apaches.

" Did you ever have any very close calls? " I asked.

He ruminated a few moments, refilled his pipe with some awful tobacco, and told the following experience:

In the time of Geronimo I was living just about where I do now; and that was just about in line with the raiding. You see, Geronimo, and Ju,[1] and old Loco used to pile out of the reservation at Camp Apache, raid south to the line, slip over into Mexico when the soldiers got too promiscuous, and raid there until they got ready to come back. Then there was always a big medicine talk. Says Geronimo:

" I am tired of the warpath. I will come back from Mexico with all my warriors, if you will escort me with soldiers and protect my people."

" All right," says the General, being only too glad to get him back at all.

So, then, in ten minutes there wouldn't be a buck in camp, but next morning they shows up again, each with about fifty head of hosses.

[1] Pronounced " Hoo."

"Where'd you get those hosses?" asks the General, suspicious.

"Had 'em pastured in the hills," answers Geronimo.

"I can't take all those hosses with me; I believe they're stolen!" says the General.

"My people cannot go without their hosses," says Geronimo.

So, across the line they goes, and back to the reservation. In about a week there's fifty-two frantic Greasers wanting to know where's their hosses. The army is nothing but an importer of stolen stock, and knows it, and can't help it.

Well, as I says, I'm between Camp Apache and the Mexican line, so that every raiding party goes right on past me. The point is that I'm a thousand feet or so above the valley, and the renegades is in such a devil of a hurry about that time that they never stop to climb up and collect me. Often I've watched them trailing down the valley in a cloud of dust. Then, in a day or two, a squad of soldiers would come up and camp at my spring for a while. They used to send soldiers to guard every water hole in the country so the renegades couldn't get water.

After a while, from not being bothered none, I got
to thinking I wasn't worth while with them.

Me and Johnny Hooper were pecking away at
the Ole Virginia mine then. We'd got down about
sixty feet, all timbered, and was thinking of cross-
cutting. One day Johnny went to town, and that same
day I got in a hurry and left my gun at camp.

I worked all the morning down at the bottom of
the shaft, and when I see by the sun it was getting
along towards noon, I put in three good shots,
tamped 'em down, lit the fusees, and started to climb
out.

It ain't noways pleasant to light a fuse in a shaft,
and then have to climb out a fifty-foot ladder, with
it burning behind you. I never did get used to it.
You keep thinking, " Now suppose there's a flaw in
that fuse, or something, and she goes off in six seconds instead of two minutes? where'll you be then? "
It would give you a good boost towards your home
on high, anyway.

So I climbed fast, and stuck my head out the top
without looking—and then I froze solid enough.
There, about fifty feet away, climbing up the hill on
mighty tired hosses, was a dozen of the ugliest Chiri-

cahuas you ever don't want to meet, and in addition
a Mexican renegade named Maria, who was worse
than any of 'em. I see at once their hosses was tired
out, and they had a notion of camping at my water
hole, not knowing nothing about the Ole Virginia
mine.

For two bits I'd have let go all holts and dropped
backwards, trusting to my thick head for easy light-
ing. Then I heard a little fizz and sputter from below.
At that my hair riz right up so I could feel the breeze
blow under my hat. For about six seconds I stood
there like an imbecile, grinning amiably. Then one
of the Chiricahuas made a sort of grunt, and I sabed
that they'd seen the original exhibit your Uncle Jim
was making of himself.

Then that fuse gave another sputter and one of
the Apaches said "Un dah." That means "white
man." It was harder to turn my head than if I'd had
a stiff neck; but I managed to do it, and I see that
my ore dump wasn't more than ten foot away. I
mighty near overjumped it; and the next I knew I
was on one side of it and those Apaches on the other.
Probably I flew; leastways I don't seem to remember
jumping.

That didn't seem to do me much good. The renegades were grinning and laughing to think how easy a thing they had; and I couldn't rightly think up any arguments against that notion—at least from their standpoint. They were chattering away to each other in Mexican for the benefit of Maria. Oh, they had me all distributed, down to my suspender buttons! And me squatting behind that ore dump about as formidable as a brush rabbit!

Then, all at once, one of my shots went off down in the shaft.

" Boom! " says she, plenty big; and a slather of rocks and stones come out of the mouth, and began to dump down promiscuous on the scenery. I got one little one in the shoulder-blade, and found time to wish my ore dump had a roof. But those renegades caught it square in the thick of trouble. One got knocked out entirely for a minute, by a nice piece of country rock in the head.

" Otra vez! " yells I, which means " again."

" Boom! " goes the Ole Virginia prompt as an answer.

I put in my time dodging, but when I gets a

chance to look, the Apaches has all got to cover, and is looking scared.

"Otra vez!" yells I again.

"Boom!" says the Ole Virginia.

This was the biggest shot of the lot, and she surely cut loose. I ought to have been half-way up the hill watching things from a safe distance, but I wasn't. Lucky for me the shaft was a little on the drift, so she didn't quite shoot my way. But she distributed about a ton over those renegades. They sort of half got to their feet uncertain.

"Otra vez!" yells I once more, as bold as if I could keep her shooting all day.

It was just a cold, raw blazer; and if it didn't go through I could see me as an Apache parlour ornament. But it did. Those Chiricahuas give one yell and skipped. It was surely a funny sight, after they got aboard their war ponies, to see them trying to dig out on horses too tired to trot.

I didn't stop to get all the laughs, though. In fact, I give one jump off that ledge, and I lit a-running. A quarter-hoss couldn't have beat me to that shack. There I grabbed old Meat-in-the-pot and made a climb for the tall country, aiming to wait around until dark, and then to pull out for Benson. Johnny Hooper wasn't expected till next day, which was lucky. From where I lay I could see the Apaches camped out beyond my draw, and I didn't doubt they'd visited the place. Along about sunset they all left their camp, and went into the draw, so there, I thinks, I sees a good chance to make a start before dark. I dropped down from the mesa, skirted the butte, and angled down across the country. After I'd gone a half mile from the cliffs, I ran across Johnny Hooper's fresh trail headed towards camp!

My heart jumped right up into my mouth at that. Here was poor old Johnny, a day too early, with a pack-mule of grub, walking innocent as a yearling, right into the hands of those hostiles. The trail looked pretty fresh, and Benson 's a good long day with a pack animal, so I thought perhaps I might catch him before he runs into trouble. So I ran back on the trail as fast as I could make it. The sun was down by now, and it was getting dusk.

I didn't overtake him, and when I got to the top of the cañon I crawled along very cautious and took a look. Of course, I expected to see everything up in smoke, but I nearly got up and yelled when I see everything all right, and old Sukey, the pack-mule, and Johnny's hoss hitched up as peaceful as babies to the corral.

"*That's* all right!" thinks I, "they're back in their camp, and haven't discovered Johnny yet. I'll snail him out of there."

So I ran down the hill and into the shack. Johnny sat in his chair—what there was of him. He must have got in about two hours before sundown, for they'd had lots of time to put in on him. That's the reason they'd stayed so long up the draw. Poor old Johnny! I was glad it was night, and he was dead. Apaches are the worst Injuns there is for tortures. They cut off the bottoms of old man Wilkins's feet, and stood him on an ant-hill——

In a minute or so, though, my wits gets to work.

"Why ain't the shack burned?" I asks myself, " and why is the hoss and the mule tied all so peaceful to the corral?"

It didn't take long for a man who knows Injins to answer *those* conundrums. The whole thing was a trap—for me—and I'd walked into it, chuckle-headed as a prairie-dog!

With that I makes a run outside—by now it was dark—and listens. Sure enough, I hears hosses. So I makes a rapid sneak back over the trail.

Everything seemed all right till I got up to the rim-rock. Then I heard more hosses—ahead of me. And when I looked back I could see some Injuns already at the shack, and starting to build a fire outside.

In a tight fix, a man is pretty apt to get scared till all hope is gone. Then he is pretty apt to get cool and calm. That was my case. I couldn't go ahead—there was those hosses coming along the trail. I couldn't go back—there was those Injins building the fire. So I skirmished around till I got a bright star right over the trail ahead, and I trained old Meat-in-the-pot to bear on that star, and I made up my mind that when the star was darkened I'd turn loose. So I lay there a while listening. By and by the star was blotted out, and I cut loose, and old Meat-in-the-pot missed fire—she never did it before nor since—I think that cartridge——

Well, I don't know where the Injins came from, but it seemed as if the hammer had hardly clicked before three or four of them had piled on me. I put up the best fight I could, for I wasn't figuring to be caught alive, and this miss-fire deal had fooled me all along the line. They surely had a lively time. I expected every minute to feel a knife in my back, but when I didn't get it then I knew they wanted to bring me in alive, and that made me fight harder. First and last we rolled and plunged all the way from the rimrock down to the cañon-bed. Then one of the Injins sung out:

"Maria!"

And I thought of that renegade Mexican, and what I'd heard about him, and that made me fight harder yet.

But after we'd fought down to the cañon-bed, and had lost most of our skin, a half-dozen more fell on me, and in less than no time they had me tied. Then they picked me up and carried me over to where they'd built a big fire by the corral.

Uncle Jim stopped with an air of finality, and began lazily to refill his pipe. From the open mud fireplace he picked a coal. Outside, the rain, faithful to the prophecy of the wide-ringed sun, beat fitfully against the roof.

"That was the closest call I ever had," said he at last.

"But, Uncle Jim," we cried in a confused chorus, "how did you get away? What did the Indians do to you? Who rescued you?"

Uncle Jim chuckled.

"The first man I saw sitting at that fire," said he, "was Lieutenant Price of the United States Army, and by him was Tom Horn.

"'What's this?' he asks, and Horn talks to the Injins in Apache.

"'They say they've caught Maria,' translates Horn back again.

"'Maria nothing!' says Lieutenant Price. 'This is Jim Fox. I know him.'

"So they turned me loose. It seems the troops had driven off the renegades an hour before."

"And the Indians who caught you, Uncle Jim? You said they were Indians."

"Were Tonto Basin Apaches," explained the old man—"government scouts under Tom Horn."

CHAPTER TWO

THE EMIGRANTS

AFTER the rain that had held us holed up at the Double R over one day, we discussed what we should do next.

"The flats will be too boggy for riding, and anyway the cattle will be in the high country," the Cattleman summed up the situation. "We'd bog down the chuck-wagon if we tried to get back to the J. H. But now after the rain the weather ought to be beautiful. What shall we do?"

"Was you ever in the Jackson country?" asked Uncle Jim. "It's the wildest part of Arizona. It's a big country and rough, and no one lives there, and there's lots of deer and mountain lions and bear. Here's my dogs. We might have a hunt."

"Good!" said we.

We skirmished around and found a condemned army pack saddle with aparejos, and a sawbuck saddle with kyacks. On these we managed to condense our grub and utensils. There were plenty of horses,

so our bedding we bound flat about their naked bar
rels by means of the squaw-hitch. Then we started.

That day furnished us with a demonstration of
what Arizona horses can do. Our way led first
through a cañon-bed filled with rounded boulders
and rocks, slippery and unstable. Big cottonwoods
and oaks grew so thick as partially to conceal the
cliffs on either side of us. The rim-rock was mysterious with caves; beautiful with hanging gar-
dens of tree ferns and grasses growing thick in long
transverse crevices; wonderful in colour and shape.
We passed the little cañons fenced off by the rustlers
as corrals into which to shunt from the herds their
choice of beeves.

The Cattleman shook his head at them. " Many
a man has come from Texas and established a herd
with no other asset than a couple of horses and a
branding-iron," said he.

Then we worked up gradually to a divide, whence
we could see a range of wild and rugged mountains
on our right. They rose by slopes and ledges, steep
and rough, and at last ended in the thousand-foot
cliffs of the buttes, running sheer and unbroken for
many miles. During all the rest of our trip they were

to be our companions, the only constant factors in the tumult of lesser peaks, precipitous cañons, and twisted systems in which we were constantly involved.

The sky was sun-and-shadow after the rain. Each and every Arizonan predicted clearing.

"Why, it almost never rains in Arizona," said Jed Parker. "And when it does it quits before it begins."

Nevertheless, about noon a thick cloud gathered about the tops of the Galiuros above us. Almost immediately it was dissipated by the wind, but when the peaks again showed, we stared with astonishment to see that they were white with snow. It was as though a magician had passed a sheet before them the brief instant necessary to work his great transformation. Shortly the sky thickened again, and it began to rain.

Travel had been precarious before; but now its difficulties were infinitely increased. The clay subsoil to the rubble turned slippery and adhesive. On the sides of the mountains it was almost impossible to keep a footing. We speedily became wet, our hands puffed and purple, our boots sodden with the water that had trickled from our clothing into them.

"Over the next ridge," Uncle Jim promised us, "is an old shack that I fixed up seven years ago. We can all make out to get in it."

Over the next ridge, therefore, we slipped and slid, thanking the god of luck for each ten feet gained. It was growing cold. The cliffs and palisades near at hand showed dimly behind the falling rain; beyond them waved and eddied the storm mists through which the mountains revealed and concealed proportions exaggerated into unearthly grandeur. Deep in the clefts of the box cañons the streams were filling. The roar of their rapids echoed from innumerable precipices. A soft swish of water usurped the world of sound.

Nothing more uncomfortable or more magnificent could be imagined. We rode shivering. Each said to himself, "I can stand this—right now—at the present moment. Very well; I will do so, and I will refuse to look forward even five minutes to what I may have to stand," which is the true philosophy of tough times and the only effective way to endure discomfort.

By luck we reached the bottom of that cañon without a fall. It was wide, well grown with oak trees, and belly deep in rich horse feed—an ideal

place to camp were it not for the fact that a thin
sheet of water a quarter of an inch deep was flowing
over the entire surface of the ground. We spurred
on desperately, thinking of a warm fire and a chance
to steam.

The roof of the shack had fallen in, and the floor
was six inches deep in adobe mud.

We did not dismount—that would have wet our
saddles—but sat on our horses taking in the details.
Finally Uncle Jim came to the front with a suggestion.

" I know of a cave," said he, " close under a butte.
It's a big cave, but it has such a steep floor that I'm
not sure as we could stay in it; and it's back the other
side of that ridge."

" I don't know how the ridge is to get back over—
it was slippery enough coming this way—and the
cave may shoot us out into space, but I'd like to *look*
at a dry place anyway," replied the Cattleman.

We all felt the same about it, so back over the
ridge we went. About half way down the other side
Uncle Jim turned sharp to the right, and as the
" hog back " dropped behind us, we found ourselves
out on the steep side of a mountain, the perpendicu-

lar cliff over us to the right, the river roaring savagely far down below our left, and sheets of water
glazing the footing we could find among the boulders
and débris. Hardly could the ponies keep from slipping sideways on the slope, so as we proceeded
farther and farther from the solidity of the ridge
behind us, we experienced the illusion of venturing
out on a tight rope over abysses of space. Even the
feeling of danger was only an illusion, however, com-
posite of the falling rain, the deepening twilight,
and the night that had already enveloped the plunge
of the cañon below.

Finally Uncle Jim stopped just within the drip
from the cliffs.

" Here she is," said he.

We descended eagerly. A deer bounded away from
the base of the buttes. The cave ran steep, in the
manner of an inclined tunnel, far up into the dimness.
We had to dig our toes in and scramble to make way
up it at all, but we found it dry, and after a little
search discovered a foot-ledge of earth sufficiently
broad for a seat.

" That's all right," quoth Jed Parker. " Now, for
sleeping places."

We scattered. Uncle Jim and Charley promptly annexed the slight overhang of the cliff whence the deer had jumped. It was dry at the moment, but we uttered pessimistic predictions if the wind should change. Tom Rich and Jim Lester had a little tent, and insisted on descending to the cañon-bed.

"Got to cook there, anyways," said they, and departed with the two pack mules and their bed horse.

That left the Cattleman, Windy Bill, Jed Parker, and me. In a moment Windy Bill came up to us whispering and mysterious.

"Get your cavallos and follow me," said he.

We did so. He led us two hundred yards to another cave, twenty feet high, fifteen feet in diameter, level as a floor.

"How's that?" he cried in triumph. "Found her just now while I was rustling nigger-heads for a fire."

We unpacked our beds with chuckles of joy, and spread them carefully within the shelter of the cave. Except for the very edges, which did not much matter, our blankets and "so-guns," protected by the canvas "tarp," were reasonably dry. Every once in a while a spasm of conscience would seize one or the other of us.

"It seems sort of mean on the other fellows," ruminated Jed Parker.

"They had their first choice," cried we all.

"Uncle Jim's an old man," the Cattleman pointed out.

But Windy Bill had thought of that. "I told him of this yere cave first. But he allowed he was plumb satisfied."

We finished laying out our blankets. The result looked good to us. We all burst out laughing.

"Well, I'm sorry for those fellows," cried the Cattleman.

We hobbled our horses and descended to the gleam of the fire, like guilty conspirators. There we ate hastily of meat, bread and coffee, merely for the sake of sustenance. It certainly amounted to little in the way of pleasure. The water from the direct rain, the shivering trees, and our hat brims accumulated in our plates faster than we could bail it out. The dishes were thrust under a canvas. Rich and Lester decided to remain with their tent, and so we saw them no more until morning.

We broke off back-loads of mesquite and toiled up the hill, tasting thickly the high altitude in the severe labour. At the big cave we dumped down our burdens, transported our fuel piecemeal to the vicinity of the narrow ledge, built a good fire, sat in a row, and lit our pipes. In a few moments the blaze was burning high, and our bodies had ceased shivering. Fantastically the firelight revealed the knobs and crevices, the ledges and the arching walls. Their shadows leaped, following the flames, receding and advancing like playful beasts. Far above us was a single tiny opening through which the smoke was sucked as through a chimney. The glow ruddied the men's features. Outside was thick darkness, and the swish and rush and roar of rising waters. Listening, Windy Bill was reminded of a story. We leaned back comfortably against the sloping walls of the cave, thrust our feet toward the blaze, smoked, and hearkened to the tale of Windy Bill.

There's a tur'ble lot of water running loose here, but I've seen the time and place where even what is in that drip would be worth a gold mine. That was in the emigrant days. They used to come over south of here, through what they called Emigrant Pass, on their way to Californy. I was a kid then, about eighteen year old, and what I didn't know about Injins and Agency cattle wasn't a patch of alkali. I had a kid outfit of h'ar bridle, lots of silver and such, and I used to ride over and be the handsome boy before such outfits as happened along.

They were queer people, most of 'em from Missoury and such-like southern seaports, and they were tur'ble sick of travel by the time they come in sight of Emigrant Pass. Up to Santa Fé they mostly hiked along any old way, but once there they herded up together in bunches of twenty wagons or so, 'count of our old friends Geronimo and Loco. A good many of 'em had horned cattle to their wagons, and they crawled along about two miles an hour, hotter'n hell with the blower on, nothin' to look at but a mountain a week away, chuck full of alkali, plenty of sage-brush and rattlesnakes—but mighty little water.

Why, you boys know that country down there. Between the Chiricahua Mountains and Emigrant Pass it's maybe a three or four days' journey for these yere bull-skinners.

Mostly they filled up their bellies and their kegs, hopin' to last through, but they sure found it drier than cork legs, and generally long before they hit the Springs their tongues was hangin' out a foot. You see, for all their plumb nerve in comin' so far, the most of them didn't know sic 'em. They were plumb innocent in regard to savin' their water, and Injins, and such; and the long-haired buckskin fakes they picked up at Santa Fé for guides wasn't much better.

That was where Texas Pete made his killin'.

Texas Pete was a tough citizen from the Lone Star. He was about as broad as he was long, and wore all sorts of big whiskers and black eyebrows. His heart was very bad. You never *could* tell where Texas Pete was goin' to jump next. He was a side-winder and a diamond-back and a little black rattle-snake all rolled into one. I believe that Texas Pete person cared about as little for killin' a man as for takin' a drink—and he shorely drank without an effort. Peaceable citizens just spoke soft and minded their own business; onpeaceable citizens Texas Pete used to plant out in the sage-brush.

Now this Texas Pete happened to discover a water

hole right out in the plumb middle of the desert. He promptly annexed said water hole, digs her out, timbers her up, and lays for emigrants. He charged two bits a head—man or beast—and nobody got a mouthful till he paid up in hard coin.

Think of the wads he raked in! I used to figure it up, just for the joy of envyin' him, I reckon. An average twenty-wagon outfit, first and last, would bring him in somewheres about fifty dollars—and besides he had forty-rod at four bits a glass. And outfits at that time were thicker'n spatter.

We used all to go down sometimes to watch them come in. When they see that little canvas shack and that well, they begun to cheer up and move fast. And when they see that sign, " Water, two bits a head," their eyes stuck out like two raw oysters.

Then come the kicks. What a howl they did raise, shorely. But it didn't do no manner of good. Texas Pete didn't do nothin' but sit there and smoke, with a kind of sulky gleam in one corner of his eye. He didn't even take the trouble to answer, but his Winchester lay across his lap. There wasn't no humour in the situation for him.

"How much is your water for humans?" asks one emigrant.

"Can't you read that sign?" Texas Pete asks him.

"But you don't mean two bits a head for *humans!*" yells the man. "Why, you can get whisky for that!"

"You can read the sign, can't you?" insists Texas Pete.

"I can read it all right?" says the man, tryin' a new deal, "but they tell me not to believe more'n half I read."

But that don't go; and Mr. Emigrant shells out with the rest.

I didn't blame them for raisin' their howl. Why, at that time the regular water holes was chargin' five cents a head from the government freighters, and the motto was always "Hold up Uncle Sam," at that. Once in a while some outfit would get mad and go chargin' off dry; but it was a long, long way to the Springs, and mighty hot and dusty. Texas Pete and his one lonesome water hole shorely did a big business.

Late one afternoon me and Gentleman Tim we

joggin' along above Texas Pete's place. It was a
tur'ble hot day—you had to prime yourself to spit—
and we was just gettin' back from drivin' some beef
up to the troops at Fort Huachuca. We was due to
cross the Emigrant Trail—she's wore in tur'ble deep
—you can see the ruts to-day. When we topped the
rise we see a little old outfit just makin' out to drag
along.

It was one little schooner all by herself, drug
along by two poor old cavallos that couldn't have
pulled my hat off. Their tongues was out, and every
once in a while they'd stick in a chuck-hole. Then a
man would get down and put his shoulder to the
wheel, and everybody'd take a heave, and up they'd
come, all a-trembling and weak.

Tim and I rode down just to take a look at the
curiosity.

A thin-lookin' man was drivin', all humped up.

" Hullo, stranger," says I, " ain't you 'fraid of
Injins? "

" Yes," says he.

" Then why are you travellin' through an Injin
country all alone? "

" Couldn't keep up," says he. " Can I get water
here? "

"I reckon," I answers.

He drove up to the water trough there at Texas Pete's, me and Gentleman Tim followin' along because our trail led that way. But he hadn't more'n stopped before Texas Pete was out.

"Cost you four bits to water them hosses," says he.

The man looked up kind of bewildered.

"I'm sorry," says he, "I ain't got no four bits. I got my roll lifted off'n me."

"No water, then," growls Texas Pete back at him.

The man looked about him helpless.

"How far is it to the next water?" he asks me.

"Twenty mile," I tells him.

"My God!" he says, to himself-like.

Then he shrugged his shoulders very tired.

"All right. It's gettin' the cool of the evenin'; we'll make it." He turns into the inside of that old schooner. "Gi' me the cup, Sue."

A white-faced woman who looked mighty good to us alkalis opened the flaps and gave out a tin cup, which the man pointed out to fill.

"How many of you is they?" asks Texas Pete.

"Three," replies the man, wondering.

"Well, six bits, then," says Texas Pete, "cash down."

At that the man straightens up a little.

"I ain't askin' for no water for my stock," says he, "but my wife and baby has been out in this sun all day without a drop of water. Our cask slipped a hoop and bust just this side of Dos Cabesas. The poor kid is plumb dry."

"Two bits a head," says Texas Pete.

At that the woman comes out, a little bit of a baby in her arms. The kid had fuzzy yellow hair, and its face was flushed red and shiny.

"Shorely you won't refuse a sick child a drink of water, sir," says she.

But Texas Pete had some sort of a special grouch; I guess he was just beginning to get his snowshoes off after a fight with his own forty-rod.

"What the hell are you-all doin' on the trail without no money at all?" he growls, "and how do you expect to get along? Such plumb tenderfeet drive me weary."

"Well," says the man, still reasonable, "I ain't got no money, but I'll give you six bits' worth of flour or trade or an'thin' I got."

"I don't run no truck store," snaps Texas Pete, and turns square on his heel and goes back to his chair.

"Got six bits about you?" whispers Gentleman Tim to me.

"Not a red," I answers.

Gentleman Tim turns to Texas Pete.

"Let 'em have a drink, Pete. I'll pay you next time I come down."

"Cash down," growls Pete.

"You're the meanest man I ever see," observes Tim. "I wouldn't speak to you if I met you in hell carryin' a lump of ice in your hand."

"You're the softest *I* ever see," sneers Pete. "Don't they have any genooine Texans down your way?"

"Not enough to make it disagreeable," says Tim.

"That lets you out," growls Pete, gettin' hostile and handlin' of his rifle.

Which the man had been standin' there bewildered, the cup hangin' from his finger. At last, lookin' pretty desperate, he stooped down to dig up a little of the wet from an overflow puddle lyin' at his feet. At the same time the hosses, left sort of to themselves, and bein' drier than a covered bridge, drug forward and stuck their noses in the trough.

Gentleman Tim and me was sittin' there on our hosses, a little to one side. We saw Texas Pete jump up from his chair, take a quick aim, and cut loose with his rifle. It was plumb unexpected to us. We hadn't thought of any shootin', and our six-shooters was tied in, 'count of the jumpy country we'd been drivin' the steers over. But Gentleman Tim, who had unslung his rope, aimin' to help the hosses out of the chuck-hole, snatched her off the horn, and with one of the prettiest twenty-foot flip throws I ever see done he snaked old Texas Pete right out of his wicky-up, gun and all. The old renegade did his best to twist around for a shot at us; but it was no go; and I never enjoyed hog-tying a critter more in my life than I enjoyed hog-tying Texas Pete. Then we turned to see what damage had been done.

We were some relieved to find the family all right, but Texas Pete had bored one of them poor old crow-bait hosses plumb through the head.

"It's lucky for you you don't get the old man," says Gentleman Tim very quiet and polite.

Which Gentleman Tim was an Irishman, and I'd

been on the range long enough with him to know that when he got quiet and polite it was time to dodge behind something.

"I hope, sir," says he to the stranger, "that you will give your wife and baby a satisfying drink. As for your hoss, pray do not be under any apprehension. Our friend, Mr. Texas Pete, here, has kindly consented to make good any deficiencies from his own corral."

Tim could talk high, wide, and handsome when he set out to.

The man started to say something; but I managed to herd him to one side.

"Let him alone," I whispers. "When he talks that way, he's mad; and when he's mad, it's better to leave nature to supply the lightnin' rods."

He seemed to sabe all right, so we built us a little fire and started some grub, while Gentleman Tim walked up and down very grand and fierce.

By and by he seemed to make up his mind. He went over and untied Texas Pete.

"Stand up, you hound," says he. "Now listen to me. If you make a break to get away, or if you refuse to do just as I tell you, I won't shoot you, but I'll

march you up country and see that Geronimo gets
you."

He sorted out a shovel and pick, made Texas Pete
carry them right along the trail a quarter, and
started him to diggin' a hole.

Texas Pete started in hard enough, Tim sittin'
over him on his hoss, his six-shooter loose, and his
rope free. The man and I stood by, not darin' to
say a word. After a minute or so Texas Pete began
to work slower and slower. By and by he stopped.

"Look here," says he, "is this here thing my
grave?"

"I am goin' to see that you give the gentleman's
hoss decent interment," says Gentleman Tim very
polite.

"Bury a hoss!" growls Texas Pete.

But he didn't say any more. Tim cocked his six-
shooter.

"Perhaps you'd better quit panting and sweat a
little," says he.

Texas Pete worked hard for a while, for Tim's
quietness was beginning to scare him up the worst
way. By and by he had got down maybe four or five
feet, and Tim got off his hoss.

"I think that will do," says he. "You may come

out. Billy, my son, cover him. Now, Mr. Texas Pete," he says, cold as steel, "there is the grave. We will place the hoss in it. Then I intend to shoot you and put you in with the hoss, and write you an epitaph that will be a comfort to such travellers of the Trail as are honest, and a warnin' to such as are not. I'd as soon kill you now as an hour from now, so you may make a break for it if you feel like it."

He stooped over to look in the hole. I thought he looked an extra long time, but when he raised his head his face had changed complete.

"March!" says he very brisk.

We all went back to the shack. From the corral Tim took Texas Pete's best team and hitched her to the old schooner.

"There," says he to the man. "Now you'd better hit the trail. Take that whisky keg there for water. Good-bye."

We sat there without sayin' a word for some time after the schooner had pulled out. Then Tim says very abrupt:

"I've changed my mind."

He got up.

"Come on, Billy," says he to me. "We'll just leave our friend tied up. I'll be back to-morrow to turn you loose. In the meantime it won't hurt you a bit to be a little uncomfortable, and hungry—and thirsty."

We rode off just about sundown, leavin' Texas Pete lashed tight.

Now all this knocked me hell-west and crooked, and I said so, but I couldn't get a word out of Gentleman Tim. All the answer I could get was just little laughs.

We drawed into the ranch near midnight, but next mornin' Tim had a long talk with the boss, and the result was that the whole outfit was instructed to arm up with a pick or a shovel apiece, and to get set for Texas Pete's. We got there a little after noon, turned the old boy out—without firearms—and then began to dig at a place Tim told us to, near that grave of Texas Pete's. In three hours we had the finest water-hole developed you ever want to see. Then the boss stuck up a sign that said:

PUBLIC WATER-HOLE.   WATER FREE.

"Now you old skin," says he to Texas Pete, "charge all you want to on your own property. But if I ever hear of your layin' claim to this other hole, I'll shore make you hard to catch."

Then we rode off home.

You see, when Gentleman Tim inspected that grave, he noted indications of water; and it struck him that runnin' the old renegade out of business was a neater way of gettin' even than merely killin' him.

Somebody threw a fresh mesquite on the fire. The flames leaped up again, showing a thin trickle of water running down the other side of the cave. The steady downpour again made itself prominent through the re-established silence.

"What did Texas Pete do after that?" asked the Cattleman.

"Texas Pete?" chuckled Windy Bill. "Well, he put in a heap of his spare time lettin' Tim alone."

CHAPTER THREE

THE REMITTANCE MAN

AFTER Windy Bill had finished his story we began to think it time to turn in. Uncle Jim and Charley slid and slipped down the chute-like passage leading from the cave and disappeared in the direction of the overhang beneath which they had spread their bed. After a moment we tore off long bundles of the nigger-head blades, lit the resinous ends at our fire, and with these torches started to make our way along the base of the cliff to the other cave.

Once without the influence of the fire our impromptu links cast an adequate light. The sheets of rain became suddenly visible as they entered the circle of illumination. By careful scrutiny of the footing I gained the entrance to our cave without mishap. I looked back. Here and there irregularly gleamed and spluttered my companions' torches. Across each slanted the rain. All else was of inky blackness except where, between them and me, a faint red reflection shone on the wet rocks. Then I turned inside.

Now, to judge from the crumbling powder of the footing, that cave had been dry since Noah. In fact, its roof was nearly a thousand feet thick. But since we had spread our blankets, the persistent waters had soaked down and through. The thousand-foot roof had a sprung a leak. Three separate and distinct streams of water ran as from spigots. I lowered my torch. The canvas tarpaulin shone with wet, and in its exact centre glimmered a pool of water three inches deep and at least two feet in diameter.

"Well, I'll be——" I began. Then I remembered those three wending their way along a wet and disagreeable trail, happy and peaceful in anticipation of warm blankets and a level floor. I chuckled and sat on my heels out of the drip.

First came Jed Parker, his head bent to protect the fire in his pipe. He gained the very centre of the cave before he looked up. Then he cast one glance at each bed, and one at me. His grave, hawk-like features relaxed. A faint grin appeared under his long moustache. Without a word he squatted down beside me.

Next the Cattleman. He looked about him with

a comical expression of dismay, and burst into a
hearty laugh.

"I believe I said I was sorry for those other fellows," he remarked.

Windy Bill was the last. He stooped his head to
enter, straightened his lank figure, and took in the
situation without expression.

"Well, this is handy," said he; "I was gettin'
tur'ble dry, and was thinkin' I would have to climb
'way down to the creek in all this rain."

He stooped to the pool in the centre of the tarpaulin and drank.

But now our torches began to run low. A small
dry bush grew near the entrance. We ignited it, and
while it blazed we hastily sorted a blanket apiece and
tumbled the rest out of the drip.

Our return without torches along the base of that
butte was something to remember. The night was so
thick you could feel the darkness pressing on you;
the mountain dropped abruptly to the left, and was
strewn with boulders and blocks of stone. Collisions
and stumbles were frequent. Once I stepped off a
little ledge five or six feet high—nothing worse than
a barked shin. And all the while the rain, pelting us

unmercifully, searched out what poor little remnants of dryness we had been able to retain.

At last we opened out the gleam of fire in our cave, and a minute later were engaged in struggling desperately up the slant that brought us to our ledge and the slope on which our fire burned.

" My Lord! " panted Windy Bill, " a man had ought to have hooks on his eyebrows to climb up here ! "

We renewed the fire—and blessed the back-loads of mesquite we had packed up earlier in the evening. Our blankets we wrapped around our shoulders, our feet we hung over the ledge toward the blaze, our backs we leaned against the hollow slant of the cave's wall. We were not uncomfortable. The beat of the rain sprang up in the stillness, growing louder and louder, like horsemen passing on a hard road. Gradually we dozed off.

For a time everything was pleasant. Dreams came fused with realities; the firelight faded from consciousness or returned fantastic to our half-awakening; a delicious numbness overspread our tired bodies. The shadows leaped, became solid, monstrous. We fell asleep.

After a time the fact obtruded itself dimly through
our stupor that the constant pressure of the hard
rock had impeded our circulation. We stirred un-
easily, shifting to a better position. That was the beginning of awakening. The new position did not suit.
A slight shivering seized us, which the drawing closer
of the blanket failed to end. Finally I threw aside
my hat and looked out. Jed Parker, a vivid patch-
work comforter wrapped about his shoulders, stood
upright and silent by the fire. I kept still, fearing
to awaken the others. In a short time I became aware
that the others were doing identically the same thing.
We laughed, threw off our blankets, stretched, and
fed the fire.

A thick acrid smoke filled the air. The Cattleman,
rising, left a trail of incandescent footprints. We
investigated hastily, and discovered that the supposed
earth on the slant of the cave was nothing more than
bat guano, tons of it. The fire, eating its way beneath, had rendered untenable its immediate vicinity.
We felt as though we were living over a volcano.
How soon our ledge, of the same material, might be
attacked, we had no means of knowing. Overcome
with drowsiness, we again disposed our blankets, re-

solved to get as many naps as possible before even these constrained quarters were taken from us.

This happened sooner and in a manner otherwise than we had expected. Windy Bill brought us to consciousness by a wild yell. Consciousness reported to us a strange, hurried sound like the long roll on a drum. Investigation showed us that this cave, too, had sprung a leak; not with any premonitory drip, but all at once, as though someone had turned on a faucet. In ten seconds a very competent streamlet six inches wide had eroded a course down through the guano, past the fire and to the outer slope. And by the irony of fate that one—and only one—leak in all the roof expanse of a big cave was directly over one end of our tiny ledge. The Cattleman laughed.

"Reminds me of the old farmer and his kind friend," said he. "Kind friend hunts up the old farmer in the village.

"'John,' says he, 'I've sad news for you. Your barn has burned up.'

"'My Lord!' says the farmer.

"'But that ain't the worst. Your cow was burned, too.'

"'My Lord!' says the farmer.

"'But that ain't the worst. Your horses were burned.'

"'My Lord!' says the farmer.

"'But that ain't the worst. The barn set fire to the house, and it was burned—total loss.'

"'My Lord!' groans the farmer.

"'But that ain't the worst. Your wife and child were killed, too.'

"At that the farmer began to roar with laughter.

"'Good heavens, man!' cries his friend, astonished, 'what in the world do you find to laugh at in that?'

"'Don't you see?' answers the farmer. 'Why, it's so darn *complete!*'

"Well," finished the Cattleman, "that's what strikes me about our case; it's so darn complete!"

"What time is it?" asked Windy Bill.

"Midnight," I announced.

"Lord! Six hours to day!" groaned Windy Bill. "How'd you like to be doin' a nice quiet job at gardenin' in the East where you could belly up to the bar reg'lar every evenin', and drink a pussy cafe and smoke tailor-made cigareets?"

" You wouldn't like it a bit," put in the Cattleman with decision; whereupon in proof he told us the following story:

Windy has mentioned Gentleman Tim, and that reminded me of the first time I ever saw him. He was an Irishman all right, but he had been educated in England, and except for his accent he was more an Englishman than anything else. A freight outfit brought him into Tucson from Santa Fé and dumped him down on the plaza, where at once every idler in town gathered to quiz him.

Certainly he was one of the greenest specimens I ever saw in this country. He had on a pair of balloon pants and a Norfolk jacket, and was surrounded by a half-dozen baby trunks. His face was red-cheeked and aggressively clean, and his eye limpid as a child's. Most of those present thought that indicated child-ishness; but I could see that it was only utter self-unconsciousness.

It seemed that he was out for big game, and intended to go after silver-tips somewhere in these very mountains. Of course he was offered plenty of advice, and would probably have made engagements

much to be regretted had I not taken a strong fancy
to him.

" My friend," said I, drawing him aside, " I don't
want to be inquisitive, but what might you do when
you're home? "

" I'm a younger son," said he.

I was green myself in those days, and knew nothing of primogeniture.

" That is a very interesting piece of family history," said I, " but it does not answer my question."

He smiled.

" Well now, I hadn't thought of that," said he,
" but in a manner of speaking, it does. I do nothing."

" Well," said I, unabashed, " if you saw me trying
to be a younger son and likely to forget myself and
do something without meaning to, wouldn't you be
apt to warn me? "

" Well, 'pon honour, you're a queer chap. What
do you mean? "

" I mean that if you hire any of those men to
guide you in the mountains, you'll be outrageously
cheated, and will be lucky if you're not gobbled by
Apaches."

" Do you do any guiding yourself, now? " he asked,
most innocent of manner.

But I fired up.

"You damn ungrateful pup," I said, "go to the devil in your own way," and turned square on my heel.

But the young man was at my elbow, his hand on my shoulder.

"Oh, I say now, I'm sorry. I didn't rightly understand. Do wait one moment until I dispose of these boxes of mine, and then I want the honour of your further acquaintance."

He got some Greasers to take his trunks over to the hotel, then linked his arm in mine most engagingly.

"Now, my dear chap," said he, "let's go somewhere for a B & S, and find out about each other."

We were both young and expansive. We exchanged views, names, and confidences, and before noon we had arranged to hunt together, I to collect the outfit.

The upshot of the matter was that the Honourable Timothy Clare and I had a most excellent month's excursion, shot several good bear, and returned to Tucson the best of friends.

At Tucson was Schiefflein and his stories of a big strike down in the Apache country. Nothing would

do but that we should both go to see for ourselves.
We joined the second expedition; crept in the gullies,
tied bushes about ourselves when monumenting
corners, and so helped establish the town of Tombstone. We made nothing, nor attempted to. Neither
of us knew anything of mining, but we were both
thirsty for adventure, and took a schoolboy delight
in playing the game of life or death with the Chiricahuas.

In fact, I never saw anybody take to the wild life
as eagerly as the Honourable Timothy Clare. He
wanted to attempt everything. With him it was no
sooner see than try, and he had such an abundance of
enthusiasm that he generally succeeded. The balloon
pants soon went. In a month his outfit was irre-
proachable. He used to study us by the hour,
taking in every detail of our equipment, from the
smallest to the most important. Then he asked questions. For all his desire to be one of the country, he
was never ashamed to acknowledge his ignorance.

"Now, don't you chaps think it silly to wear such
high heels to your boots?" he would ask. "It seems
to me a very useless sort of vanity."

"No vanity about it, Tim," I explained. "In the

We joined the second expedition

first place, it keeps your foot from slipping through the stirrup. In the second place, it is good to grip on the ground when you are roping afoot."

" By Jove, that's true! " he cried.

So he'd get him a pair of boots. For a while it was enough to wear and own all these things. He seemed to delight in his six-shooter and his rope just as ornaments to himself and horse. But he soon got over that. Then he had to learn to use them.

For the time being, pistol practice, for instance, would absorb all his thoughts. He'd bang away at intervals all day, and figure out new theories all night.

" That bally scheme won't work," he would complain. " I believe if I extended my thumb along the cylinder, it would help that side jump."

He was always easing the trigger-pull, or filing the sights. In time he got to be a fairly accurate and very quick shot.

The same way with roping and hog-tying and all the rest.

" What's the use? " I used to ask him. " If you were going to be a buckeroo, you couldn't go into harder training."

" I like it," was always his answer.

He had only one real vice, that I could see. He would gamble. Stud poker was his favourite; and I never saw a Britisher yet who could play poker. I used to head him off when I could, and he was always grateful, but the passion was strong.

After we got back from founding Tombstone I was busted and had to go to work.

" I've got plenty," said Tim, " and it's all yours."

" I know, old fellow," I told him, " but your money wouldn't do for me."

Buck Johnson was just seeing his chance then, and was preparing to take some breeding cattle over into the Soda Springs Valley. Everybody laughed at him —said it was right in the line of the Chiricahua raids, which was true. But Buck had been in there with Agency steers, and thought he knew. So he collected a trail crew, brought some Oregon cattle across, and built his home ranch of three-foot adobe walls with portholes. I joined the trail crew; and somehow or another the Honourable Timothy got permission to go along on his own hook.

The trail was a long one. We had thirst and heat and stampedes and some Indian scares. But in the queer atmospheric conditions that prevailed that summer, I never saw the desert more wonderful. It was like waking to the glory of God to sit up at dawn and see the colours change on the dry ranges

At the home ranch, again, Tim managed to get permission to stay on. He kept his own mount of horses, took care of them, hunted, and took part in all the cow work. We lost some cattle from Indians, of course, but it was too near the Reservation for them to do more than pick up a few stray head on their way through. The troops were always after them full jump, and so they never had time to round up the beef. But of course we had to look out or we'd lose our hair, and many a cowboy has won out to the home ranch in an almighty exciting race. This was nuts for the Honourable Timothy Clare, much better than hunting silver-tips, and he enjoyed it no limit.

Things went along that way for some time, until one evening as I was turning out the horses a buckboard drew in, and from it descended Tony Briggs and a dapper little fellow dressed all in black and with a plug hat.

"Which I accounts for said hat reachin' the

ranch, because it's Friday and the boys not in town," Tony whispered to me.

As I happened to be the only man in sight, the stranger addressed me.

"I am looking," said he in a peculiar, sing-song manner I have since learned to be English, "for the Honourable Timothy Clare. Is he here?"

"Oh, you're looking for him, are you?" said I. "And who might you be?"

You see, I liked Tim, and I didn't intend to deliver him over into trouble.

The man picked a pair of eye-glasses off his stomach where they dangled at the end of a chain, perched them on his nose, and stared me over. I must have looked uncompromising, for after a few seconds he abruptly wrinkled his nose so that the glasses fell promptly to his stomach again, felt in his waistcoat pocket, and produced a card. I took it, and read:

JEFFRIES CASE, *Barrister.*

"A lawyer!" said I suspiciously.

"My dear man," he rejoined with a slight impatience, "I am not here to do your young friend a harm. In fact, my firm have been his family solicitors for generations."

"Very well," I agreed, and led the way to the one-room adobe that Tim and I occupied.

If I had expected an enthusiastic greeting for the boyhood friend from the old home, I would have been disappointed. Tim was sitting with his back to the door reading an old magazine. When we entered he glanced over his shoulder.

"Ah, Case," said he, and went on reading. After a moment he said without looking up, " Sit down."

The little man took it calmly, deposited himself in a chair and his bag between his feet, and looked about him daintily at our rough quarters. I made a move to go, whereupon Tim laid down his magazine, yawned, stretched his arms over his head, and sighed.

"Don't go, Harry," he begged. "Well, Case," he addressed the barrister, "what is it this time? Must be something devilish important to bring you —how many thousand miles is it—into such a country as this."

"It is important, Mr. Clare," stated the lawyer in his dry sing-song tones; "but my journey might have been avoided had you paid some attention to my letters."

" Letters!" repeated Tim, opening his eyes. " My dear chap, I've had no letters."

" Addressed as usual to your New York bankers."

Tim laughed softly. " Where they are, with my last two quarters' allowance. I especially instructed them to send me no mail. One spends no money in this country." He paused, pulling his moustache. " I'm truly sorry you had to come so far," he continued, " and if your business is, as I suspect, the old one of inducing me to return to my dear uncle's arms, I assure you the mission will prove quite fruitless. Uncle Hillary and I could never live in the same county, let alone the same house."

" And yet your uncle, the Viscount Mar, was very fond of you," ventured Case. " Your allowances——"

" Oh, I grant you his generosity in *money* affairs——"

" He has continued that generosity in the terms of his will, and those terms I am here to communicate to you."

" Uncle Hillary is dead!" cried Tim.

" He passed away the sixteenth of last June."

A slight pause ensued.

" I am ready to hear you," said Tim soberly, at last.

The barrister stooped and began to fumble with his bag.

" No, not that!" cried Tim, with some impatience. " Tell me in your own words."

The lawyer sat back and pressed his finger points together over his stomach.

" The late Viscount," said he, " has been graciously pleased to leave you in fee simple his entire estate of Staghurst, together with its buildings, rentals, and privileges. This, besides the residential rights, amounts to some ten thousands pounds sterling per annum."

" A little less than fifty thousand dollars a year, Harry," Tim shot over his shoulder at me.

" There is one condition," put in the lawyer.

" Oh, there is!" exclaimed Tim, his crest falling. " Well, knowing my Uncle Hillary——"

" The condition is not extravagant," the lawyer hastily interposed. " It merely entails continued residence in England, and a minimum of nine months on the estate. This provision is absolute, and the estate reverts on its discontinuance, but may I be permitted to observe that the majority of men, myself among the number, are content to spend the most of their lives, not merely in the confines of a kingdom, but between the four walls of a room, for much less than ten thousand pounds a year. Also that England is not without its attractions for an Englishman, and that Staghurst is a country place of many possibilities."

The Honourable Timothy had recovered from his first surprise.

" And if the condition is not complied with? " he inquired.

" Then the estate reverts to the heirs at law, and you receive an annuity of one hundred pounds, payable quarterly."

" May I ask further the reason for this extraordinary condition? "

" My distinguished client never informed me," replied the lawyer, " but "—and a twinkle appeared in his eye— " as an occasional disburser of funds— Monte Carlo——"

Tim burst out laughing.

" Oh, but I recognise Uncle Hillary there! " he

cried. "Well, Mr. Case, I am sure Mr. Johnson, the owner of this ranch, can put you up, and to-morrow we'll start back."

He returned after a few minutes to find me sitting smoking a moody pipe. I liked Tim, and I was sorry to have him go. Then, too, I was ruffled, in the senseless manner of youth, by the sudden altitude to which his changed fortunes had lifted him. He stood in the middle of the room, surveying me, then came across and laid his arm on my shoulder.

"Well," I growled, without looking up, "you're a very rich man now, Mr. Clare."

At that he jerked me bodily out of my seat and stood me up in the centre of the room, the Irish blazing out of his eyes.

"Here, none of that!" he snapped. "You damn little fool! Don't you 'Mr. Clare' me!"

So in five minutes we were talking it over. Tim was very much excited at the prospect. He knew Staghurst well, and told me all about the big stone house, and the avenue through the trees; and the hedge-row roads, and the lawn with its peacocks, and the round green hills, and the labourers' cottages.

"It's home," said he, "and I didn't realise before

how much I wanted to see it. And I'll be a man of weight there, Harry, and it'll be mighty good."

We made all sorts of plans as to how I was going to visit him just as soon as I could get together the money for the passage. He had the delicacy not to offer to let me have it; and that clinched my trust and love of him.

The next day he drove away with Tony and the dapper little lawyer. I am not ashamed to say that I watched the buckboard until it disappeared in the mirage.

I was with Buck Johnson all that summer, and the following winter, as well. We had our first round-up, found the natural increase much in excess of the loss by Indians, and extended our holdings up over the Rock Creek country. We witnessed the start of many Indian campaigns, participated in a few little brushes with the Chiricahuas, saw the beginning of the cattle-rustling. A man had not much opportunity to think of anything but what he had right on hand, but I found time for a few speculations on Tim. I wondered how he looked now, and what he was doing, and how in blazes he managed to get away with fifty thousand a year.

And then one Sunday in June, while I was lying on my bunk, Tim pushed open the door and walked in. I was young, but I'd seen a lot, and I knew the expression of his face. So I laid low and said nothing.

In a minute the door opened again, and Buck Johnson himself came in.

"How do," said he; "I saw you ride up."

"How do you do," replied Tim.

"I know all about you," said Buck, without any preliminaries; "your man, Case, has wrote me. I don't know your reasons, and I don't want to know —it's none of my business—and I ain't goin' to tell you just what kind of a damn fool I think you are —that's none of my business, either. But I want you to understand without question how you stand on the ranch."

"Quite good, sir," said Tim very quietly.

"When you were out here before I was glad to have you here as a sort of guest. Then you were what I've heerd called a gentleman of leisure. Now you're nothin' but a remittance man. Your money's nothin' to me, but the principle of the thing is. The country is plumb pestered with remittance men, doin'

nothin', and I don't aim to run no home for incom-
petents. I had a son of a duke drivin' wagon for
me; and he couldn't drive nails in a snow-bank. So
don't you herd up with the idea that you can come
on this ranch and loaf."

"I don't want to loaf," put in Tim, "I want a
job."

"I'm willing to give you a job," replied Buck,
"but it's jest an ordinary cow-puncher's job at
forty a month. And if you don't fill your saddle,
it goes to someone else."

"That is satisfactory," agreed Tim.

"All right," finished Buck, "so that's understood.
Your friend Case wanted me to give you a lot of
advice. A man generally has about as much use for
advice as a cow has for four hind legs."

He went out.

"For God's sake, what's up?" I cried, leaping
from my bunk.

"Hullo, Harry," said he, as though he had seen
me the day before, "I've come back."

"How come back?" I asked. "I thought you
couldn't leave the estate. Have they broken the
will?"

"No," said he.

"Is the money lost?"

"No."

"Then what?"

"The long and short of it is, that I couldn't afford that estate and that money."

"What do you mean?"

"I've given it up."

"Given it up! What for?"

"To come back here."

I took this all in slowly.

"Tim Clare," said I at last, "do you mean to say that you have given up an English estate and fifty thousand dollars a year to be a remittance man at five hundred, and a cow-puncher on as much more?"

"Exactly," said he.

"Tim," I adjured him solemnly, "you are a damn fool!"

"Maybe," he agreed.

"Why did you do it?" I begged.

He walked to the door and looked out across the desert to where the mountains hovered like soap-bubbles on the horizon. For a long time he looked; then whirled on me.

"Harry," said he in a low voice, "do you remember the camp we made on the shoulder of the mountain that night we were caught out? And do you remember how the dawn came up on the big snow peaks across the way—and all the cañon below us filled with whirling mists—and the steel stars leaving us one by one? Where could I find room for that in English paddocks? And do you recall the day we trailed across the Yuma deserts, and the sun beat into our skulls, and the dry, brittle hills looked like papier-maché, and the grey sage-bush ran off into the rise of the hills; and then came sunset and the hard, dry mountains grew filmy, like gauze veils of many colours, and melted and glowed and faded to slate blue, and the stars came out? The English hills are rounded and green and curried, and the sky is near, and the stars only a few miles up. And do you recollect that dark night when old Loco and his warriors were camped at the base of Cochise's Stronghold, and we crept down through the velvet dark wondering when we would be discovered, our mouths sticky with excitement, and the little winds blowing? "

He walked up and down a half-dozen times, his breast heaving.

" It's all very well for the man who is brought
up to it, and who has seen nothing else. Case can
exist in four walls; he has been brought up to it
and knows nothing different. But a man like me——

" They wanted me to canter between hedge-rows
—I who have ridden the desert where the sky over
me and the plain under me were bigger than the
Islander's universe! They wanted me to oversee little
farms—I who have watched the sun rising over half
a world! Talk of your ten thou' a year, and what
it'll buy! You know, Harry, how it feels when
a steer takes the slack of your rope, and your pony
sits back! Where in England can I buy that? You
know the rising and the falling of days, and the
boundless spaces where your heart grows big, and
the thirst of the desert and the hunger of the trail,
and a sun that shines and fills the sky, and a wind
that blows fresh from the wide places! Where in
parcelled, snug, green, tight little England could
I buy that with ten thou'—aye, or an hundred times
ten thou'? No, no, Harry, that fortune would cost
me too dear. I have seen and done and been too
much. I've come back to the Big Country, where the
pay is poor and the work is hard and the comfort

small, but where a man and his soul meet their Maker face to face."

The Cattleman had finished his yarn. For a time no one spoke. Outside, the volume of rain was subsiding. Windy Bill reported a few stars shining through rifts in the showers. The chill that precedes the dawn brought us as close to the fire as the smouldering guano would permit.

" I don't know whether he was right or wrong," mused the Cattleman, after a while. " A man can do a heap with that much money. And yet an old ' alkali ' is never happy anywhere else. However," he concluded emphatically, " one thing I do know: rain, cold, hunger, discomfort, curses, kicks, and violent deaths included, there isn't one of you grumblers who would hold that gardening job you spoke of three days! "

CHAPTER FOUR

THE CATTLE RUSTLERS

Dawn broke, so we descended through wet grasses to the cañon. There, after some difficulty, we managed to start a fire, and so ate breakfast, the rain still pouring down on us. About nine o'clock, with miraculous suddenness, the torrent stopped. It began to turn cold. The Cattleman and I decided to climb to the top of the butte after meat, which we entirely lacked.

It was rather a stiff ascent, but once above the sheer cliffs we found ourselves on a rolling meadow tableland, a half-mile broad by, perhaps, a mile and a half in length. Grass grew high; here and there were small live oaks planted park-like; slight and rounded ravines accommodated brooklets. As we walked back, the edges blended in the edges of the mesa across the cañon. The deep gorges, which had heretofore seemed the most prominent elements of the scenery, were lost. We stood, apparently, in the middle of a wide and undulating plain, diversified by little ridges, and running with a free sweep to the very foot of the snowy Galiuros. It seemed as though we should be able to ride horseback in almost any given direction. Yet we knew that ten minutes' walk would take us to the brink of most stupendous chasms—so deep that the water flowing in them hardly seemed to move; so rugged that only with the greatest difficulty could a horseman make his way through the country at all; and yet so ancient that the bottoms supported forests, rich grasses, and rounded, gentle knolls. It was a most astonishing set of double impressions.

We succeeded in killing a nice, fat white-tail buck, and so returned to camp happy. The rain held off. We dug ditches, organised shelters, cooked a warm meal. For the next day we planned a bear hunt afoot, far up a manzañita cañon where Uncle Jim knew of some "holing up" caves.

But when we awoke in the morning we threw aside our coverings with some difficulty to look on a ground covered with snow; trees laden almost to the breaking point with snow, and the air filled with it.

" No bear to-day," said the Cattleman.

" No," agreed Uncle Jim drily. " No b'ar. And what's more, unless yo're aimin' to stop here somewhat of a spell, we'll have to make out to-day."

We cooked with freezing fingers, ate while dodging avalanches from the trees, and packed reluctantly. The ropes were fozen, the hobbles stiff, everything either crackling or wet. Finally the task was finished. We took a last warming of the fingers and climbed on.

The country was wonderfully beautiful with the white not yet shaken from the trees and rock ledges. Also it was wonderfully slippery. The snow was soft enough to ball under the horses' hoofs, so that most of the time the poor animals skated and stumbled along on stilts. Thus we made our way back over ground which, naked of these difficulties, we had considered bad enough. Imagine riding along a slant of rock shelving off to a bad tumble, so steep that your pony has to do more or less expert ankle work to keep from slipping off sideways. During the passage of that rock you are apt to sit very light. Now cover it with several inches of snow, stick a snowball on each hoof of your mount, and

try again. When you have ridden it—or its dupli•
cate—a few score of times, select a steep mountain
side, cover it with round rocks the size of your head,
and over that spread a concealing blanket of the
same sticky snow. You are privileged to vary these
to the limits of your imagination.

Once across the divide, we ran into a new sort
of trouble. You may remember that on our journey
over we had been forced to travel for some distance
in a narrow stream-bed. During our passage we
had scrambled up some rather steep and rough
slopes, and hopped up some fairly high ledges.
Now we found the heretofore dry bed flowing a
good eight inches deep. The steep slopes had become cascades; the ledges, waterfalls. When we came
to them we had to " shoot the rapids " as best we
could, only to land with a *plunk* in an indetermi-
nately deep pool at the bottom. Some of the pack
horses went down, sousing again our unfortunate
bedding, but by the grace of fortune not a saddle
pony lost his feet.

After a time the gorge widened. We came out
into the box cañon with its trees. Here the water
spread and shoaled to a depth of only two or three

inches. We splashed along gaily enough, for, with the exception of an occasional quicksand or boggy spot, our troubles were over.

Jed Parker and I happened to ride side by side, bringing up the rear and seeing to it that the pack animals did not stray or linger. As we passed the first of the rustlers' corrals, he called my attention to them.

"Go take a look," said he. "We only got those fellows out of here two years ago."

I rode over. At this point the rim-rock broke to admit the ingress of a ravine into the main cañon. Riding a short distance up the ravine, I could see that it ended abruptly in a perpendicular cliff. As the sides also were precipitous, it became necessary only to build a fence across the entrance into the main cañon to become possessed of a corral completely closed in. Remembering the absolute invisibility of these sunken cañons until the rider is almost directly over them, and also the extreme roughness and remoteness of the district, I could see that the spot was admirably adapted to concealment.

"There's quite a yarn about the gang that held

this hole," said Jed Parker to me, when I had ridden back to him. " I'll tell you about it sometime."

We climbed the hill, descended on the Double R, built a fire in the stove, dried out, and were happy. After a square meal—and a dry one—I reminded Jed Parker of his promise, and so, sitting cross-legged on his " so-gun " in the middle of the floor, he told us the following yarn:

There's a good deal of romance been written about the " bad man," and there's about the same amount of nonsense. The bad man is just a plain murderer, neither more nor less. He never does get into a real, good, plain, stand-up gun fight if he can possibly help it. His killin's are done from behind a door, or when he's got his man dead to rights. There's Sam Cook. You've all heard of him. He had nerve, of course, and when he was backed into a corner he made good; and he was sure sudden death with a gun. But when he went out for a man deliberate, he didn't take no special chances. For a while he was marshal at Willets. Pretty soon it was noted that there was a heap of cases of resisting arrest, where Sam as marshal had to shoot, and that those

cases almost always happened to be his personal
enemies. Of course, that might be all right, but it
looked suspicious. Then one day he killed poor old
Max Schmidt out behind his own saloon. Called him
out and shot him in the stomach. Said Max resisted
arrest on a warrant for keepin' open out of hours!
That was a sweet warrant to take out in Willets,
anyway! Mrs. Schmidt always claimed that she saw
that deal played, and that, while they were talkin'
perfectly peaceable, Cook let drive from the hip
at about two yards' range. Anyway, we decided we
needed another marshal. Nothin' else was ever done,
for the Vigilantes hadn't been formed, and your individual and decent citizen doesn't care to be marked
by a bad man of that stripe. Leastways, unless he
wants to go in for bad-man methods and do a little
ambusheein' on his own account.

The point is, that these yere bad men are a low-
down, miserable proposition, and plain, cold-blood
murderers, willin' to wait for a sure thing, and without no compunctions whatever. The bad man takes
you unawares, when you're sleepin', or talkin', or
drinkin', or lookin' to see what for a day it's goin'
to be, anyway. He don't give you no show, and

sooner or later he's goin' to get you in the safest and easiest way for himself. There ain't no romance about that.

And, until you've seen a few men called out of their shacks for a friendly conversation, and shot when they happen to look away; or asked for a drink of water, and killed when they stoop to the spring; or potted from behind as they go into a room, it's pretty hard to believe that any man can be so plumb lackin' in fair play or pity or just natural humanity.

As you boys know, I come in from Texas to Buck Johnson's about ten year back. I had a pretty good mount of ponies that I knew, and I hated to let them go at prices they were offerin' then, so I made up my mind to ride across and bring them in with me. It wasn't so awful far, and I figured that I'd like to take in what New Mexico looked like anyway.

About down by Albuquerque I tracked up with another outfit headed my way. There was five of them, three men, and a woman, and a yearlin' baby. They had a dozen hosses, and that was about all I could see. There was only two packed, and no wagon. I suppose the whole outfit—pots, pans, and kettles—was worth five dollars. It was just supper when I run across them, and it didn't take more'n one look to discover that flour, coffee, sugar, and salt was all they carried. A yearlin' carcass, half-skinned, lay near, and the fry-pan was full of meat.

"Howdy, strangers," says I, ridin' up.

They nodded a little, but didn't say nothin'. My hosses fell to grazin', and I eased myself around in my saddle, and made a cigareet. The men was tall, lank fellows, with kind of sullen faces, and sly, shifty eyes; the woman was dirty and generally mussed up. I knowed that sort all right. Texas was gettin' too many fences for them.

"Havin' supper?" says I, cheerful.

One of 'em grunted "Yes" at me; and, after a while, the biggest asked me very grudgin' if I wouldn't light and eat, I told them "No," that I was travellin' in the cool of the evenin'.

"You seem to have more meat than you need, though," says I. "I could use a little of that."

"Help yourself," says they. "It's a maverick we come across."

I took a steak, and noted that the hide had been

mighty well cut to ribbons around the flanks, and that the head was gone.

"Well," says I to the carcass, "no one's goin' to be able to swear whether you're a maverick or not, but I bet you knew the feel of a brandin' iron all right."

I gave them a thank-you, and climbed on again. My hosses acted some surprised at bein' gathered up again, but I couldn't help that.

"It looks like a plumb imposition, cavallos," says I to them, "after an all-day, but you sure don't want to join that outfit any more than I do the angels, and if we camp here we're likely to do both."

I didn't see them any more after that until I'd hit the Lazy Y, and had started in runnin' cattle in the Soda Springs Valley. Larry Eagen and me rode together those days, and that's how I got to know him pretty well. One day, over in the Elm Flat, we ran smack on this Texas outfit again, headed north. This time I was on my own range, and I knew where I stood, so I could show a little more curiosity in the case.

"Well, you got this far," says I.

"Yes," says they.

"Where you headed?"

"Over towards the hills."

"What to do?"

"Make a ranch, raise some truck; perhaps buy a few cows."

They went on.

"Truck farmin'," says I to Larry, "is fine prospects in this country."

He sat on his horse lookin' after them.

"I'm sorry for them," says he. "It must be almighty hard scratchin'."

Well, we rode the range for upwards of two year. In that time we saw our Texas friends—name of Hahn—two or three times in Willets, and heard of them off and on. They bought an old brand of Steve McWilliams for seventy-five dollars, carryin' six or eight head of cows. After that, from time to time, we heard of them buyin' more—two or three head from one man, and two or three from another. They branded them all with that McWilliams iron —T O—so, pretty soon, we began to see the cattle on the range.

Now, a good cattleman knows cattle just as well as you know people, and he can tell them about as far off. Horned critters look alike to you, but even in a country supportin' a good many thousand head, a man used to the business can recognise most every individual as far as he can see him. Some is better than others at it. I suppose you really have to be brought up to it. So we boys at the Lazy Y noted all the cattle with the new T O, and could estimate pretty close that the Hahn outfit might own, maybe, thirty-five head all told.

That was all very well, and nobody had any kick comin'. Then, one day in the spring, we came across our first "sleeper."

What's a sleeper? A sleeper is a calf that has been ear-marked, but not branded. Every owner has a certain brand, as you know, and then he crops and slits the ears in a certain way, too. In that manner he don't have to look at the brand, except to corroborate the ears; and, as the critter generally sticks his ears up inquirin'-like to anyone ridin' up, it's easy to know the brand without lookin' at it, merely from the ear-marks. Once in a great while, when a man comes across an unbranded calf, and it ain't handy to build a fire, he just ear-marks it and let's the brandin' go till later. But it isn't done often, and our outfit had strict orders never to make sleepers.

Well, one day in the spring, as I say, Larry and me was ridin', when we came across a Lazy Y cow and calf. The little fellow was ear-marked all right, so we rode on, and never would have discovered nothin' if a bush rabbit hadn't jumped and scared the calf right across in front of our hosses. Then we couldn't help but see that there wasn't no brand.

Of course we roped him and put the iron on him. I took the chance to look at his ears, and saw that the marking had been done quite recent, so when we got in that night I reported to Buck Johnson that one of the punchers was gettin' lazy and sleeperin'. Naturally he went after the man who had done it; but every puncher swore up and down, and back and across, that he'd branded every calf he'd had a rope on that spring. We put it down that someone was lyin', and let it go at that.

And then, about a week later, one of the other boys reported a Triangle-H sleeper. The Triangle-H was the Goodrich brand, so we didn't have nothin' to do with that. Some of them might be sleeperin'

for all we knew. Three other cases of the same kind
we happened across that same spring.

So far, so good. Sleepers runnin' in such numbers
was a little astonishin', but nothin' suspicious. Cattle did well that summer, and when we come to round
up in the fall, we cut out maybe a dozen of those
T O cattle that had strayed out of that Hahn country. Of the dozen there was five grown cows, and
seven yearlin's.

"My Lord, Jed," says Buck to me, "they's a
heap of these youngsters comin' over our way."

But still, as a young critter is more apt to stray
than an old one that's got his range established, we
didn't lay no great store by that neither. The Hahns
took their bunch, and that's all there was to it.

Next spring, though, we found a few more sleepers, and one day we came on a cow that had gone
dead lame. That was usual, too, but Buck, who was
with me, had somethin' on his mind. Finally he
turned back and roped her, and threw her.

"Look here, Jed," says he, "what do you make
of this?"

I could see where the hind legs below the hocks
had been burned.

"Looks like somebody had roped her by the hind feet," says I.

"Might be," says he, "but her bein' lame that way makes it look more like hobbles."

So we didn't say nothin' more about that neither, until just by luck we came on another lame cow. We threw her, too.

"Well, what do you think of this one?" Buck Johnson asks me.

"The feet is pretty well tore up," says I, "and down to the quick, but I've seen them tore up just as bad on the rocks when they come down out of the mountains."

You sabe what that meant, don't you? You see, a rustler will take a cow and hobble her, or lame her so she can't follow, and then he'll take her calf a long ways off and brand it with his iron. Of course, if we was to see a calf of one brand followin' of a cow with another, it would be just too easy to guess what had happened.

We rode on mighty thoughtful. There couldn't be much doubt that cattle rustlers was at work. The sleepers they had ear-marked, hopin' that no one would discover the lack of a brand. Then, after the calf was weaned, and quit followin' of his mother, the rustler would brand it with his own iron, and change its ear-mark to match. It made a nice, easy way of gettin' together a bunch of cattle cheap.

But it was pretty hard to guess off-hand who the rustlers might be. There were a lot of renegades down towards the Mexican line who made a raid once in a while, and a few oilers [1] livin' near had water holes in the foothills, and any amount of little cattle holders, like this T O outfit, and any of them wouldn't shy very hard at a little sleeperin' on the side. Buck Johnson told us all to watch out, and passed the word quiet among the big owners to try and see whose cattle seemed to have too many calves for the number of cows.

The Texas outfit I'm tellin' you about had settled up above in this Double R cañon where I showed you those natural corrals this morning. They'd built them a 'dobe, and cleared some land, and planted a few trees, and made an irrigated patch for alfalfa. Nobody never rode over his way very much, 'cause the country was most too rough for cattle, and our ranges lay farther to the southward. Now, however, we began to extend our ridin' a little. I was down

[1] "Oilers"—Greasers—Mexicans.

towards Dos Cabesas to look over the cattle there, and they used to send Larry up into the Double R country. One evenin' he took me to one side.

"Look here, Jed," says he, "I know you pretty well, and I'm not ashamed to say that I'm all new at this cattle business—in fact, I haven't been at it more'n a year. What should be the proportion of cows to calves anyhow?"

"There ought to be about twice as many cows as there're calves," I tells him.

"Then, with only about fifty head of grown cows, there ought not to be an equal number of yearlin's?"

"I should say not," says I. "What are you drivin' at?"

"Nothin' yet," says he.

A few days later he tackled me again.

"Jed," says he, "I'm not good, like you fellows are, at knowin' one cow from another, but there's a calf down there branded T O that I'd pretty near swear I saw with an X Y cow last month. I wish you could come down with me."

We got that fixed easy enough, and for the next month rammed around through this broken country,

lookin' for evidence. I saw enough to satisfy me to
a moral certainty, but nothin' for a sheriff; and, of
course, we couldn't go shoot up a peaceful rancher
on mere suspicion. Finally, one day, we run on a
four-months' calf all by himself, with the T O iron
onto him—a mighty healthy lookin' calf, too.

"Wonder where *his* mother is!" says I.

"Maybe it's a ' dogie,' " says Larry Eagen—we
calls calves whose mothers have died " dogies."

"No," says I, " I don't hardly think so. A dogie
is always under size and poor, and he's layin' around
water holes, and he always has a big, sway belly
onto him. No, this is no dogie; and, if it's an honest
calf, there sure ought to be a T O cow around somewhere."

So we separated to have a good look. Larry
rode up on the edge of a little rim-rock. In a minute
I saw his hoss jump back, dodgin' a rattlesnake
or somethin', and then fall back out of sight. I
jumped my hoss up there tur'ble quick, and looked
over, expectin' to see nothin' but mangled remains.
It was only about fifteen foot down, but I couldn't
see bottom 'count of some brush.

I saw his horse jump back dodgin' a rattlesnake or somethin'

" Are you all right? " I yells.

" Yes, yes! " cries Larry, " but for the love of God get down here as quick as you can."

I hopped off my hoss and scrambled down some-how.

" Hurt? " says I, as soon as I lit.

" Not a bit—look here."

There was a dead cow with the Lazy Y on her flank.

" And a bullet-hole in her forehead," adds Larry. " And, look here, that T O calf was bald-faced, and so was this cow."

" Reckon we found our sleepers," says I.

So, there we was. Larry had to lead his cavallo down the barranca to the main cañon. I followed along on the rim, waitin' until a place gave me a chance to get down, too, or Larry a chance to get up. We were talkin' back and forth when, all at once, Larry shouted again.

" Big game this time," he yells. " Here's a cave and a mountain lion squallin' in it."

I slid down to him at once, and we drew our six-shooters and went up to the cave openin', right under the rim-rock. There, sure enough, were fresh lion tracks, and we could hear a little faint cryin' like a woman.

"First chance," claims Larry, and dropped to his hands and knees at the entrance.

"Well, damn me!" he cries, and crawls in at once, payin' no attention to me tellin' him to be more cautious. In a minute he backs out, carryin' a three-year-old girl.

"We seem to be in for adventures to-day," says he. "Now, where do you suppose that came from, and how did it get here?"

"Well," says I, "I've followed lion tracks where they've carried yearlin's across their backs like a fox does a goose. They're tur'ble strong."

"But where did she come from?" he wonders.

"As for that," says I, "don't you remember now that T O outfit had a yearlin' kid when it came into the country?"

"That's right," says he. "It's only a mile down the cañon. I'll take it home. They must be most distracted about it."

So I scratched up to the top where my pony was waitin'. It was a tur'ble hard climb, and I 'most had to have hooks on my eyebrows to get up at all. It's easier to slide down than to climb back. I dropped my gun out of my holster, and she went way to the bottom, but I wouldn't have gone back for six guns. Larry picked it up for me.

So we went along, me on the rim-rock and around the barrancas, and Larry in the bottom carryin' of the kid.

By and by we came to the ranch house, stopped to wait. The minute Larry hove in sight everybody was out to once, and in two winks the woman had that baby. They didn't see me at all, but I could hear, plain enough, what they said. Larry told how he had found her in the cave, and all about the lion tracks, and the woman cried and held the kid close to her, and thanked him about forty times. Then when she'd wore the edge off a little, she took the kid inside to feed it or somethin'.

"Well," says Larry, still laughin', "I must hit the trail."

"You say you found her up the Double R?" asks Hahn. "Was it that cave near the three cotton-woods?"

"Yes," says Larry.

"Where'd you get into the cañon?"

"Oh, my hoss slipped off into the barranca just above."

"The barranca just above," repeats Hahn, lookin' straight at him.

Larry took one step back.

"You ought to be almighty glad I got into the cañon at all," says he.

Hahn stepped up, holdin' out his hand.

"That's right," says he. "You done us a good turn there."

Larry took his hand. At the same time Hahn pulled his gun and shot him through the middle.

It was all so sudden and unexpected that I stood there paralysed. Larry fell forward the way a man mostly will when he's hit in the stomach, but somehow he jerked loose a gun and got it off twice. He didn't hit nothin', and I reckon he was dead before he hit the ground. And there he had my gun, and I was about as useless as a pocket in a shirt!

No, sir, you can talk as much as you please, but the killer is a low-down ornery scub, and he don't hesitate at no treachery or ingratitude to keep his carcass safe.

Jed Parker ceased talking. The dusk had fallen in the little room, and dimly could be seen the recumbent figures lying at ease on their blankets. The ranch foreman was sitting bolt upright, cross-legged. A faint glow from his pipe barely distinguished his features.

" What became of the rustlers? " I asked him.

" Well, sir, that is the queer part. Hahn himself, who had done the killin', skipped out. We got out warrants, of course, but they never got served. He was a sort of half outlaw from that time, and was killed finally in the train hold-up of '97. But the others we tried for rustling. We didn't have much of a case, as the law went then, and they'd have gone free if the woman hadn't turned evidence against them. The killin' was too much for her. And, as the precedent held good in a lot of other rustlin' cases, Larry's death was really the beginnin' of law and order in the cattle business."

We smoked. The last light suddenly showed red against the grimy window. Windy Bill arose and looked out the door.

" Boys," said he, returning, " she's cleared off. We can get back to the ranch to-morrow."

CHAPTER FIVE

THE DRIVE

A CRY awakened me. It was still deep night. The moon sailed overhead, the stars shone unwavering like candles, and a chill breeze wandered in from the open spaces of the desert. I raised myself on my elbow, throwing aside the blankets and the canvas tarpaulin. Forty other indistinct, formless bundles on the ground all about me were sluggishly astir. Four figures passed and repassed between me and a red fire. I knew them for the two cooks and the horse wranglers. One of the latter was grumbling.

" Didn't git in till moon-up last night," he growled. " Might as well trade my bed for a lantern and be done with it."

Even as I stretched my arms and shivered a little, the two wranglers threw down their tin plates with a clatter, mounted horses and rode away in the direction of the thousand acres or so known as the pasture.

I pulled on my clothes hastily, buckled in my buckskin shirt, and dove for the fire. A dozen others were before me. It was bitterly cold. In the east the sky had paled the least bit in the world, but the moon and stars shone on bravely and undiminished. A band of coyotes was shrieking desperate blas·phemies against the new day, and the stray herd, awakening, was beginning to bawl and bellow.

Two crater-like dutch ovens, filled with pieces of fried beef, stood near the fire; two galvanised water buckets, brimming with soda biscuits, flanked them; two tremendous coffee pots stood guard at either end. We picked us each a tin cup and a tin plate from the box at the rear of the chuck wagon; helped ourselves from a dutch oven, a pail, and a coffee pot, and squatted on our heels as close to the fire as possible. Men who came too late borrowed the shovel, scooped up some coals, and so started little fires of their own about which new groups formed.

While we ate, the eastern sky lightened. The mountains under the dawn looked like silhouettes cut from slate-coloured paper; those in the west showed faintly luminous. Objects about us became dimly visible. We could make out the windmill, and the adobe of the ranch houses, and the corrals. The cowboys arose one by one, dropped their plates into the dishpan, and began to hunt out their ropes. Everything was obscure and mysterious in the faint grey light. I watched Windy Bill near his tarpaulin. He stooped to throw over the canvas. When he bent, it was before daylight; when he straightened his back, daylight had come. It was just like that, as though someone had reached out his hand to turn on the illumination of the world.

The eastern mountains were fragile, the plain was ethereal, like a sea of liquid gases. From the pasture we heard the shoutings of the wranglers, and made out a cloud of dust. In a moment the first of the remuda came into view, trotting forward with the free grace of the unburdened horse. Others followed in procession: those near sharp and well defined, those in the background more or less obscured by the dust, now appearing plainly, now fading like ghosts. The leader turned unhesitatingly into the corral. After him poured the stream of the remuda—two hundred and fifty saddle horses—with an unceasing thunder of hoofs.

Immediately the cook-camp was deserted. The cowboys entered the corral. The horses began to circle around the edge of the enclosure as around the circumference of a circus ring. The men, grouped at the centre, watched keenly, looking for the mounts they had already decided on. In no time each had recognised his choice, and, his loop trailing, was walking toward that part of the revolving circumference where his pony dodged. Some few whirled the loop, but most cast it with a quick flip. It was really marvellous to observe the accuracy with which the noose would fly, past a dozen tossing heads, and over a dozen backs, to settle firmly about the neck of an animal perhaps in the very centre of the group. But again, if the first throw failed, it was interesting to see how the selected pony would dodge, double back, twist, turn, and hide to escape a second cast. And it was equally interesting to observe how his companions would help him. They seemed to realise that they were not wanted, and would push themselves between the cowboy and his intended mount with the utmost boldness. In the thick dust that instantly arose, and with the bewildering thunder of galloping, the flashing change

of grouping, the rush of the charging animals, rec-
ognition alone would seem almost impossible, yet in
an incredibly short time each had his mount, and the
others, under convoy of the wranglers, were meekly
wending their way out over the plain. There, until
time for a change of horses, they would graze in
a loose and scattered band, requiring scarcely any
supervision. Escape? Bless you, no, that thought
was the last in their minds.

In the meantime the saddles and bridles were
adjusted. Always in a cowboy's " string " of from
six to ten animals the boss assigns him two or three
broncos to break in to the cow business. Therefore,
each morning we could observe a half dozen or so
men gingerly leading wicked looking little animals
out to the sand " to take the pitch out of them."
One small black, belonging to a cowboy called the
Judge, used more than to fulfil expectations of a
good time.

" Go to him, Judge! " someone would always remark.

" If he ain't goin' to pitch, I ain't goin' to make
him," the Judge would grin, as he swung aboard.

The black would trot off quite calmly and in a

most matter of fact way, as though to shame all slanderers of his lamb-like character. Then, as the bystanders would turn away, he would utter a squeal, throw down his head, and go at it. He was a very hard bucker, and made some really spectacular jumps, but the trick on which he based his claims to originality consisted in standing on his hind legs at so perilous an approach to the perpendicular that his rider would conclude he was about to fall backwards, and then suddenly springing forward in a series of stiff-legged bucks. The first manœuvre induced the rider to loosen his seat in order to be ready to jump from under, and the second threw him before he could regain his grip.

"And they say a horse don't think!" exclaimed an admirer.

But as these were broken horses—save the mark! —the show was all over after each had had his little fling. We mounted and rode away, just as the mountain peaks to the west caught the rays of a sun we should not enjoy for a good half hour yet.

I had five horses in my string, and this morning rode "that C S horse, Brown Jug." Brown Jug was a powerful and well-built animal, about fourteen

two in height, and possessed of a vast enthusiasm
for cow-work. As the morning was frosty, he felt
good.

At the gate of the water corral we separated into
two groups. The smaller, under the direction of Jed
Parker, was to drive the mesquite in the wide flats;
the rest of us, under the command of Homer, the
round-up captain, were to sweep the country even
as far as the base of the foothills near Mount
Graham. Accordingly we put our horses to the full
gallop.

Mile after mile we thundered along at a brisk
rate of speed. Sometimes we dodged in and out
among the mesquite bushes, alternately separating
and coming together again; sometimes we swept
over grassy plains apparently of illimitable extent;
sometimes we skipped and hopped and buck-jumped
through and over little gullies, barrancas, and other
sorts of malpais—but always without drawing rein.
The men rode easily, with no thought to the way
nor care for the footing. The air came back sharp
against our faces. The warm blood stirred by the
rush flowed more rapidly. We experienced a delightful glow. Of the morning cold only the very

tips of our fingers and the ends of our noses retained a remnant. Already the sun was shining low and level across the plains. The shadows of the cañons modelled the hitherto flat surfaces of the mountains.

After a time we came to some low hills helmeted with the outcrop of a rock escarpment. Hitherto they had seemed a termination of Mount Graham, but now, when we rode around them, we discovered them to be separated from the range by a good five miles of sloping plain. Later we looked back and would have sworn them part of the Dos Cabesas system, did we not know them to be at least eight miles' distant from that rocky rampart. It is always that way in Arizona. Spaces develop of whose existence you had not the slightest intimation. Hidden in apparently plane surfaces are valleys and prairies. At one sweep of the eye you embrace the entire area of an eastern State; but nevertheless the reality as you explore it foot by foot proves to be infinitely more than the vision has promised.

Beyond the hill we stopped. Here our party divided again, half to the right and half to the left. We had ridden, up to this time, directly away from camp, now we rode a circumference of which headquarters was the centre. The country was pleasantly rolling and covered with grass. Here and there were clumps of soapweed. Far in a remote distance lay a slender dark line across the plain. This we knew to be mesquite; and once entered, we knew it, too, would seem to spread out vastly. And then this grassy slope, on which we now rode, would show merely as an insignificant streak of yellow. It is also like that in Arizona. I have ridden in succession through grass land, brush land, flower land, desert. Each in turn seemed entirely to fill the space of the plains between the mountains.

From time to time Homer halted us and detached a man. The business of the latter was then to ride directly back to camp, driving all cattle before him. Each was in sight of his right- and left-hand neighbour. Thus was constructed a drag-net whose meshes contracted as home was neared.

I was detached, when of our party only the Cattleman and Homer remained. They would take the outside. This was the post of honour, and required the hardest riding, for as soon as the cattle should realise the fact of their pursuit, they would attempt to " break " past the end and up the valley. Brown

Jug and I congratulated ourselves on an exciting morning in prospect.

Now, wild cattle know perfectly well what a drive means, and they do not intend to get into a round-up if they can help it. Were it not for the two facts, that they are afraid of a mounted man, and cannot run quite so fast as a horse, I do not know how the cattle business would be conducted. As soon as a band of them caught sight of any one of us, they curled their tails and away they went at a long, easy lope that a domestic cow would stare at in wonder. This was all very well; in fact we yelled and shrieked and otherwise uttered cow-calls to keep them going, to " get the cattle started," as they say. But pretty soon a little band of the many scurrying away before our thin line, began to bear farther and farther to the east. When in their judgment they should have gained an opening, they would turn directly back and make a dash for liberty. Accordingly the nearest cowboy clapped spurs to his horse and pursued them.

It was a pretty race. The cattle ran easily enough, with long, springy jumps that carried them over the ground faster than appearances would lead one to believe. The cow-pony, his nose stretched out, his ears slanted, his eyes snapping with joy of the chase, flew fairly "belly to earth." The rider sat slightly forward, with the cowboy's loose seat. A whirl of dust, strangely insignificant against the immensity of a desert morning, rose from the flying group. Now they disappeared in a ravine, only to scramble out again the next instant, pace undiminished. The rider merely rose slightly and threw up his elbows to relieve the jar of the rough gully. At first the cattle seemed to hold their own, but soon the horse began to gain. In a short time he had come abreast of the leading animal. The latter stopped short with a snort, dodged back, and set out at right angles to his former course. From a dead run the pony came to a stand in two fierce plunges, doubled like a shot, and was off on the other tack. An unaccustomed rider would here have lost his seat. The second dash was short. With a final shake of the head, the steers turned to the proper course in the direction of the ranch. The pony dropped unconcernedly to the shuffling jog of habitual progression.

Far away stretched the arc of our cordon. The

most distant rider was a speck, and the cattle ahead
of him were like maggots endowed with a smooth,
swift onward motion. As yet the herd had not taken
form; it was still too widely scattered. Its units, in
the shape of small bunches, momently grew in numbers. The distant plains were crawling and alive
with minute creatures making toward a common tiny
centre.

Immediately in our front the cattle at first behaved
very well. Then far down the long gentle slope I
saw a break for the upper valley. The manikin
that represented Homer at once became even smaller
as it departed in pursuit. The Cattleman moved
down to cover Homer's territory until he should return, and I in turn edged farther to the right.
Then another break from another bunch. The Cattleman rode at top speed to head it. Before long he
disappeared in the distant mesquite. I found myself
in sole charge of a front three miles long.

The nearest cattle were some distance ahead, and
trotting along at a good gait. As they had not yet
discovered the chance left open by unforeseen circumstance, I descended and took in on my cinch
while yet there was time. Even as I mounted, an im-

patient movement on the part of experienced Brown
Jug told me that the cattle had seen their opportunity.

I gathered the reins and spoke to the horse. He
needed no further direction, but set off at a wide
angle, nicely calculated, to intercept the truants.
Brown Jug was a powerful beast. The spring of
his leap was as whalebone. The yellow earth began
to stream past like water. Always the pace increased
with a growing thunder of hoofs. It seemed that
nothing could turn us from the straight line, nothing check the headlong momentum of our rush. My
eyes filled with tears from the wind of our going.
Saddle strings streamed behind. Brown Jug's mane
whipped my bridle hand. Dimly I was conscious of
soapweed, sacatone, mesquite, as we passed them.
They were abreast and gone before I could think
of them or how they were to be dodged. Two antelope bounded away to the left; birds rose hastily
from the grasses. A sudden *chirk, chirk, chirk,* rose
all about me. We were in the very centre of a prairie-
dog town, but before I could formulate in my mind
the probabilities of holes and broken legs, the *chirk,
chirk, chirk*ing had fallen astern. Brown Jug had
skipped and dodged successfully.

We were approaching the cattle. They ran stubbornly and well, evidently unwilling to be turned until the latest possible moment. A great rage at their obstinacy took possession of us both. A broad shallow wash crossed our way, but we plunged through its rocks and boulders recklessly, angered at even the slight delay they necessitated. The hard land on the other side we greeted with joy. Brown Jug extended himself with a snort.

Suddenly a jar seemed to shake my very head loose. I found myself staring over the horse's head directly down into a deep and precipitous gully, the edge of which was so cunningly concealed by the grasses as to have remained invisible to my blurred vision. Brown Jug, however, had caught sight of it at the last instant, and had executed one of the wonderful stops possible only to a cow-pony.

But already the cattle had discovered a passage above, and were scrambling down and across. Brown Jug and I, at more sober pace, slid off the almost perpendicular bank, and out the other side.

A moment later we had headed them. They whirled, and without the necessity of any suggestion on my part Brown Jug turned after them, and so quickly that my stirrup actually brushed the ground. After that we were masters. We chased the cattle far enough to start them well in the proper direction, and then pulled down to a walk in order to get a breath of air.

But now we noticed another band, back on the ground over which we had just come, doubling through in the direction of Mount Graham. A hard run set them to rights. We turned. More had poured out from the hills. Bands were crossing everywhere, ahead and behind. Brown Jug and I set to work.

Being an indivisible unit, we could chase only one bunch at a time; and, while we were after one, a half dozen others would be taking advantage of our preoccupation. We could not hold our own. Each run after an escaping bunch had to be on a longer diagonal. Gradually we were forced back, and back, and back; but still we managed to hold the line unbroken. Never shall I forget the dash and clatter of that morning. Neither Brown Jug nor I thought for a moment of sparing horseflesh, nor of picking a route. We made the shortest line, and paid little attention to anything that stood in the way. A very fever of resistance possessed us. It was like beating against a head wind, or fighting fire, or combating in any other way any of the great forces of nature. We were quite alone. The Cattleman and Homer had vanished. To our left the men were fully occupied in marshalling the compact brown herds that had gradually massed—for these antagonists of mine were merely the outlying remnants.

I suppose Brown Jug must have run nearly twenty miles with only one check. Then we chased a cow some distance and into the dry bed of a stream, where she whirled on us savagely. By luck her horn hit only the leather of my saddle skirts, so we left her; for when a cow has sense enough to " get on the peck," there is no driving her farther. We gained nothing, and had to give ground, but we succeeded in holding a semblance of order, so that the cattle did not break and scatter far and wide. The sun had by now well risen, and was beginning to shine hot. Brown Jug still ran gamely and displayed as much interest as ever, but he was evidently tiring. We were both glad to see Homer's grey showing in the fringe of mesquite.

Together we soon succeeded in throwing the cows into the main herd. And, strangely enough, as soon as they had joined a compact band of their fellows, their wildness left them and, convoyed by outsiders, they set themselves to plodding energetically toward the home ranch.

As my horse was somewhat winded, I joined the " drag " at the rear. Here by course of natural sifting soon accumulated all the lazy, gentle, and sickly cows, and the small calves. The difficulty now was to prevent them from lagging and dropping out. To that end we indulged in a great variety of the picturesque cow-calls peculiar to the cowboy. One found an old tin can which by the aid of a few pebbles he converted into a very effective rattle.

The dust rose in clouds and eddied in the sun. We slouched easily in our saddles. The cowboys compared notes as to the brands they had seen. Our ponies shuffled along, resting, but always ready for a dash in chase of an occasional bull calf or yearling with independent ideas of its own.

Thus we passed over the country, down the long gentle slope to the " sink " of the valley, whence another long gentle slope ran to the base of the other ranges. At greater or lesser distances we caught the dust, and made out dimly the masses of the other herds collected by our companions, and by the party under Jed Parker. They went forward toward the common centre, with a slow ruminative movement, and the dust they raised went with them.

Little by little they grew plainer to us, and the home ranch, hitherto merely a brown shimmer in the distance, began to take on definition as the group of buildings, windmills, and corrals we knew. Miniature horsemen could be seen galloping forward to the open white plain where the herd would be held. Then the mesquite enveloped us; and we knew little more, save the anxiety lest we overlook laggards in the brush, until we came out on the edge of that same white plain.

Here were more cattle, thousands of them, and billows of dust, and a great bellowing, and dim, mounted figures riding and shouting ahead of the herd. Soon they succeeded in turning the leaders back. These threw into confusion those that followed. In a few moments the cattle had stopped. A cordon of horsemen sat at equal distances holding them in.

"Pretty good haul," said the man next to me; "a good five thousand head."

CHAPTER SIX

CUTTING OUT

IT was somewhere near noon by the time we had bunched and held the herd of some four or five thousand head in the smooth, wide flat, free from bushes and dog holes. Each sat at ease on his horse facing the cattle, watching lazily the clouds of dust and the shifting beasts, but ready at any instant to turn back the restless or independent individuals that might break for liberty.

Out of the haze came Homer, the round-up captain, on an easy lope. As he passed successively the sentries he delivered to each a low command, but without slacking pace. Some of those spoken to wheeled their horses and rode away. The others settled themselves in their saddles and began to roll cigarettes.

"Change horses; get something to eat," said he to me; so I swung after the file trailing at a canter over the low swells beyond the plain.

108

The remuda had been driven by its leaders to a corner of the pasture's wire fence, and there held. As each man arrived he dismounted, threw off his saddle, and turned his animal loose. Then he flipped a loop in his rope and disappeared in the eddying herd. The discarded horse, with many grunts, indulged in a satisfying roll, shook himself vigorously, and walked slowly away. His labour was over for the day, and he knew it, and took not the slightest trouble to get out of the way of the men with the swinging ropes.

Not so the fresh horses, however. They had no intention of being caught, if they could help it, but dodged and twisted, hid and doubled behind the moving screen of their friends. The latter, seeming as usual to know they were not wanted, made no effort to avoid the men, which probably accounted in great measure for the fact that the herd as a body remained compact, in spite of the cowboys threading it, and in spite of the lack of an enclosure.

Our horses caught, we saddled as hastily as possible; and then at the top speed of our fresh and eager ponies we swept down on the chuck wagon. There we fell off our saddles and descended on the

meat and bread like ravenous locusts on a cornfield.
The ponies stood where we left them, " tied to the
ground " in the cattle-country fashion.

As soon as a man had stoked up for the afternoon
he rode away. Some finished before others, so across
the plain formed an endless procession of men returning to the herd, and of those whom they replaced
coming for their turn at the grub.

We found the herd quiet. Some were even lying
down, chewing their cuds as peacefully as any barn-
yard cows. Most, however, stood ruminative, or
walked slowly to and fro in the confines allotted by
the horsemen, so that the herd looked from a distance like a brown carpet whose pattern was constantly changing—a dusty brown carpet in the
process of being beaten. I relieved one of the watch-
ers, and settled myself for a wait.

At this close inspection the different sorts of cattle showed more distinctly their characteristics. The
cows and calves generally rested peacefully enough,
the calf often lying down while the mother stood
guard over it. Steers, however, were more restless.
They walked ceaselessly, threading their way in and
o ut among the standing cattle, pausing in brutish

amazement at the edge of the herd, and turning back immediately to endless journeyings. The bulls, excited by so much company forced on their accustomed solitary habit, roared defiance at each other until the air fairly trembled. Occasionally two would clash foreheads. Then the powerful animals would push and wrestle, trying for a chance to gore. The decision of supremacy was a question of but a few minutes, and a bloody topknot the worst damage. The defeated one side-stepped hastily and clumsily out of reach, and then walked away.

Most of the time all we had to do was to sit our horses and watch these things, to enjoy the warm bath of the Arizona sun, and to converse with our next neighbours. Once in a while some enterprising cow, observing the opening between the men, would start to walk out. Others would fall in behind her until the movement would become general. Then one of us would swing his leg off the pommel and jog his pony over to head them off. They would return peacefully enough.

But one black muley cow, with a calf as black and muley as herself, was more persistent. Time after time, with infinite patience, she tried it again the moment my back was turned. I tried driving her far into the herd. No use; she always returned. Quirtings and stones had no effect on her mild and steady persistence.

"She's a San Simon cow," drawled my neighbour. "Everybody knows her. She's at every round-up, just naturally raisin' hell."

When the last man had returned from chuck, Homer made the dispositions for the cut. There were present probably thirty men from the home ranches round about, and twenty representing owners at a distance, here to pick up the strays inevitable to the season's drift. The round-up captain appointed two men to hold the cow-and-calf cut, and two more to hold the steer cut. Several of us rode into the herd, while the remainder retained their positions as sentinels to hold the main body of cattle in shape.

Little G and I rode slowly among the cattle looking everywhere. The animals moved sluggishly aside to give us passage, and closed in as sluggishly behind us, so that we were always closely hemmed in wherever we went. Over the shifting sleek backs, through the eddying clouds of dust, I could make out the figures of my companions moving slowly, apparently aimlessly, here and there.

Our task for the moment was to search out the unbranded J H calves. Since in ranks so closely crowded it would be physically impossible actually to see an animal's branded flank, we depended entirely on the ear-marks.

Did you ever notice how any animal, tame or wild, always points his ears inquiringly in the direction of whatever interests or alarms him? Those ears are for the moment his most prominent feature. So when a brand is quite indistinguishable because, as now, of press of numbers, or, as in winter, from extreme length of hair, the cropped ears tell plainly the tale of ownership. As every animal is so marked when branded, it follows that an uncut pair of ears means that its owner has never felt the iron.

So, now we had to look first of all for calves with uncut ears. After discovering one, we had to ascertain his ownership by examining the ear-marks of his mother, by whose side he was sure, in this alarming multitude, to be clinging faithfully.

Calves were numerous, and J H cows everywhere to be seen, so in somewhat less than ten seconds I had

my eye on a mother and son. Immediately I turned
Little G in their direction. At the slap of my quirt
against the stirrup, all the cows immediately about
me shrank suspiciously aside. Little G stepped forward daintily, his nostrils expanding, his ears working back and forth, trying to the best of his ability
to understand which animals I had selected. The
cow and her calf turned in toward the centre of the
herd. A touch of the reins guided the pony. At once
he comprehended. From that time on he needed no
further directions. Cautiously, patiently, with great
skill, he forced the cow through the press toward
the edge of the herd. It had to be done very quietly,
at a foot pace, so as to alarm neither the objects of
pursuit nor those surrounding them. When the cow
turned back, Little G somehow happened always in
her way. Before she knew it she was at the outer
edge of the herd. There she found herself, with a
group of three or four companions, facing the open
plain. Instinctively she sought shelter. I felt Little
G's muscles tighten beneath me. The moment for action had come. Before the cow had a chance to dodge
among her companions the pony was upon her like
a thunderbolt. She broke in alarm, trying desper-

ately to avoid the rush. There ensued an exciting contest of dodgings, turnings, and doublings. Wherever she turned Little G was before her. Some of his evolutions were marvellous. All I had to do was to sit my saddle, and apply just that final touch of judgment denied even the wisest of the lower animals. Time and again the turn was so quick that the stirrup swept the ground. At last the cow, convinced of the uselessness of further effort to return, broke away on a long lumbering run to the open plain. She was stopped and held by the men detailed, and so formed the nucleus of the new cut-herd. Immediately Little G, his ears working in conscious virtue, jog-trotted back into the herd, ready for another.

After a dozen cows had been sent across to the cut-herd, the work simplified. Once a cow caught sight of this new band, she generally made directly for it, head and tail up. After the first short struggle to force her from the herd, all I had to do was to start her in the proper direction and keep her at it until her decision was fixed. If she was too soon left to her own devices, however, she was likely to return. An old cowman knows to a second just the proper moment to abandon her.

Sometimes in spite of our best efforts a cow succeeded in circling us and plunging into the main
herd. The temptation was then strong to plunge in
also, and to drive her out by main force; but the
temptation had to be resisted. A dash into the thick
of it might break the whole band. At once, of his
own accord, Little G dropped to his fast, shuffling
walk, and again we addressed ourselves to the task
of pushing her gently to the edge.

This was all comparatively simple—almost any
pony is fast enough for the calf cut—but now
Homer gave orders for the steer cut to begin, and
steers are rapid and resourceful and full of natural
cussedness. Little G and I were relieved by Windy
Bill, and betook ourselves to the outside of the herd.

Here we had leisure to observe the effects that up
to this moment we had ourselves been producing. The
herd, restless by reason of the horsemen threading it,
shifted, gave ground, expanded, and contracted, so
that its shape and size were always changing in the
constant area guarded by the sentinel cowboys. Dust
arose from these movements, clouds of it, to eddy
and swirl, thicken and dissipate in the currents of
air. Now it concealed all but the nearest dimly-out-

lined animals; again it parted in rifts through which mistily we discerned the riders moving in and out of the fog; again it lifted high and thin, so that we saw in clarity the whole herd and the outriders and the mesas far away. As the afternoon waned, long shafts of sun slanted through this dust. It played on men and beasts magically, expanding them to the dimensions of strange genii, appearing and effacing themselves in the billows of vapour from some enchanted bottle.

We on the outside found our sinecure of hot noontide filched from us by the cooler hours. The cattle, wearied of standing, and perhaps somewhat hungry and thirsty, grew more and more impatient. We rode continually back and forth, turning the slow movement in on itself. Occasionally some particularly enterprising cow would conclude that one or another of the cut-herds would suit her better than this mill of turmoil. She would start confidently out, head and tail up, find herself chased back, get stubborn on the question, and lead her pursuer a long, hard run before she would return to her companions. Once in a while one would even have to be roped and dragged back. For know, before something happens to you,

that you can chase a cow safely only until she gets
hot and winded. Then she stands her ground and
gets emphatically " on the peck."

I remember very well when I first discovered this.
It was after I had had considerable cow work, too. I
thought of cows as I had always seen them—afraid
of a horseman, easy to turn with the pony, and willing to be chased as far as necessary to the work.
Nobody told me anything different. One day we
were making a drive in an exceedingly broken country. I was bringing in a small bunch I had discovered
in a pocket of the hills, but was excessively annoyed
by one old cow that insisted on breaking back. In
the wisdom of further experience, I now conclude
that she probably had a calf in the brush. Finally
she got away entirely. After starting the bunch well
ahead, I went after her.

Well, the cow and I ran nearly side by side for as
much as half a mile at top speed. She declined to be
headed. Finally she fell down and was so entirely
winded that she could not get up.

"Now, old girl, I've got you!" said I, and set
myself to urging her to her feet.

The pony acted somewhat astonished, and suspicious of the job. Therein he knew a lot more than I did. But I insisted, and, like a good pony, he obeyed. I yelled at the cow, and slapped my hat, and used my quirt. When she had quite recovered her wind, she got slowly to her feet—and charged me in a most determined manner.

Now, a bull, or a steer, is not difficult to dodge. He lowers his head, shuts his eyes, and comes in on one straight rush. But a cow looks to see what she is doing; her eyes are open every minute, and it over-joys her to take a side hook at you even when you succeed in eluding her direct charge.

The pony I was riding did his best, but even then could not avoid a sharp prod that would have ripped him up had not my leather bastos intervened. Then we retired to a distance in order to plan further; but we did not succeed in inducing that cow to revise her ideas, so at last we left her. When, in some chagrin, I mentioned to the round-up captain the fact that I had skipped one animal, he merely laughed.

"Why, kid," said he, " you can't do nothin' with a cow that gets on the prod that away 'thout you ropes her; and what could you do with her out there if you *did* rope her?"

So I learned one thing more about cows.

After the steer cut had been finished, the men rep·
resenting the neighbouring ranges looked through
the herd for strays of their brands. These were
thrown into the stray-herd, which had been brought
up from the bottom lands to receive the new acces-
sions. Work was pushed rapidly, as the afternoon
was nearly gone.

In fact, so absorbed were we that until it was
almost upon us we did not notice a heavy thunder-
shower that arose in the region of the Dragoon
Mountains, and swept rapidly across the zenith.
Before we knew it the rain had begun. In ten seconds
it had increased to a deluge, and in twenty we were
all to leeward of the herd striving desperately to
stop the drift of the cattle down wind.

We did everything in our power to stop them,
but in vain. Slickers waved, quirts slapped against
leather, six-shooters flashed, but still the cattle, heads
lowered, advanced with a slow and sullen persistence
that would not be stemmed. If we held our ground,
they divided around us. Step by step we were forced
to give way—the thin line of nervou_'y plunging
horses sprayed before the dense mass of the cattle.

"No, they won't stampede," shouted Charley to my question. "There's cows and calves in them. If they was just steers or grown critters, they might."

The sensations of those few moments were very vivid—the blinding beat of the storm in my face, the unbroken front of horned heads bearing down on me, resistless as fate, the long slant of rain with the sun shining in the distance beyond it.

Abruptly the downpour ceased. We shook our hats free of water, and drove the herd back to the cutting grounds again.

But now the surface of the ground was slippery, and the rapid manœuvring of horses had become a matter precarious in the extreme. Time and again the ponies fairly sat on their haunches and slid when negotiating a sudden stop, while quick turns meant the rapid scramblings that only a cow-horse could accomplish. Nevertheless the work went forward unchecked. The men of the other outfits cut their cattle into the stray-herd. The latter was by now of considerable size, for this was the third week of the round-up.

Finally everyone expressed himself as satisfied. The largely diminished main herd was now started forward by means of shrill cowboy cries and beating of quirts. The cattle were only too eager to go. From my position on a little rise above the stray-herd I could see the leaders breaking into a run, their heads thrown forward as they snuffed their freedom. On the mesa side the sentinel riders quietly withdrew. From the rear and flanks the horsemen closed in. The cattle poured out in a steady stream through the opening thus left on the mesa side. The fringe of cowboys followed, urging them on. Abruptly the cavalcade turned and came loping back. The cattle continued ahead on a trot, gradually spreading abroad over the landscape, losing their integrity as a herd. Some of the slower or hungrier dropped out and began to graze. Certain of the more wary disappeared to right or left.

Now, after the day's work was practically over, we had our first accident. The horse ridden by a young fellow from Dos Cabesas slipped, fell, and rolled quite over his rider. At once the animal lunged to his feet, only to be immediately seized by the nearest rider. But the Dos Cabesas man lay still, his arms and legs spread abroad, his head doubled sideways in a horribly suggestive manner. We hopped off. Two men straightened him out, while two more looked carefully over the indications on the ground.

"All right," sang out one of these, "the horn didn't catch him."

He pointed to the indentation left by the pommel. Indeed five minutes brought the man to his senses. He complained of a very twisted back. Homer sent one of the men in after the bed-wagon, by means of which the sufferer was shortly transported to camp. By the end of the week he was again in the saddle. How men escape from this common accident with injuries so slight has always puzzled me. The horse rolls completely over his rider, and yet it seems to be the rarest thing in the world for the latter to be either killed or permanently injured.

Now each man had the privilege of looking through the J H cuts to see if by chance strays of his own had been included in them. When all had expressed themselves as satisfied, the various bands were started to the corrals.

From a slight eminence where I had paused to enjoy the evening I looked down on the scene. The three herds, separated by generous distances one from the other, crawled leisurely along; the riders, their hats thrust back, lolled in their saddles, shouting conversation to each other, relaxing after the day's work; through the clouds strong shafts of light belittled the living creatures, threw into proportion the vastness of the desert.

CHAPTER SEVEN

A CORNER IN HORSES

IT was dark night. The stray-herd bellowed fran·
tically from one of the big corrals; the cow-and-calf-
herd from a second. Already the remuda, driven in
from the open plains, scattered about the thousand
acres of pasture. Away from the conveniences of
fence and corral, men would have had to patrol all
night. Now, however, everyone was gathered about
the camp fire.

Probably forty cowboys were in the group, representing all types, from old John, who had been in
the business forty years, and had punched from the
Rio Grande to the Pacific, to the Kid, who would
have given his chance of salvation if he could have
been taken for ten years older than he was. At the
moment Jed Parker was holding forth to his friend
Johnny Stone in reference to another old crony who
had that evening joined the round-up.

"Johnny," inquired Jed with elaborate gravity,

and entirely ignoring the presence of the subject of conversation, " what is that thing just beyond the fire, and where did it come from? "

Johnny Stone squinted to make sure.

" That? " he replied. " Oh, this evenin' the dogs see something run down a hole, and they dug it out, and that's what they got."

The newcomer grinned.

" The trouble with you fellows," he proffered " is that you're so plumb alkalied you don't know the real thing when you see it."

" That's right," supplemented Windy Bill. " *He* come from New York."

" No! " cried Jed. " You don't say so? Did he come in one box or in two? "

Under cover of the laugh, the newcomer made a raid on the dutch ovens and pails. Having filled his plate, he squatted on his heels and fell to his belated meal. He was a tall, slab-sided individual, with a lean, leathery face, a sweeping white moustache, and a grave and sardonic eye. His leather chaps were plain and worn, and his hat had been fashioned by time and wear into much individuality. I was not surprised to hear him nicknamed Sacatone Bill.

"Just ask him how he got that game foot," suggested Johnny Stone to me in an undertone, so, of course, I did not.

Later someone told me that the lameness resulted from his refusal of an urgent invitation to return across a river. Mr. Sacatone Bill happened not to be riding his own horse at the time.

The Cattleman dropped down beside me a moment later.

"I wish," said he in a low voice, "we could get that fellow talking. He is a queer one. Pretty well educated apparently. Claims to be writing a book of memoirs. Sometimes he will open up in good shape, and sometimes he will not. It does no good to ask him direct, and he is as shy as an old crow when you try to lead him up to a subject. We must just lie low and trust to Providence."

A man was playing on the mouth organ. He played excellently well, with all sorts of variations and frills. We smoked in silence. The deep rumble of the cattle filled the air with its diapason. Always the shrill coyotes raved out in the mesquite. Sacatone Bill had finished his meal, and had gone to sit by Jed Parker, his old friend. They talked together

low-voiced. The evening grew, and the eastern sky
silvered over the mountains in anticipation of the
moon.

Sacatone Bill suddenly threw back his head and
laughed.

"Reminds me of the time I went to Colorado!"
he cried.

"He's off!" whispered the Cattleman.

A dead silence fell on the circle. Everybody shifted
position the better to listen to the story of Sacatone
Bill.

About ten year ago I got plumb sick of punchin'
cows around my part of the country. She hadn't
rained since Noah, and I'd forgot what water outside
a pail or a trough looked like. So I scouted around inside of me to see what part of the world I'd jump to,
and as I seemed to know as little of Colorado and
minin' as anything else, I made up the pint of bean
soup I call my brains to go there. So I catches me a
buyer at Benson and turns over my pore little bunch
of cattle and prepared to fly. The last day I hauled
up about twenty good buckets of water and threw,

her up against the cabin. My buyer was settin' his hoss waitin' for me to get ready. He didn't say nothin' until we'd got down about ten mile or so.

"Mr. Hicks," says he, hesitatin' like, "I find it a good rule in this country not to overlook other folks' plays, but I'd take it mighty kind if you'd explain those actions of yours with the pails of water."

"Mr. Jones," says I, "it's very simple. I built that shack five year ago, and it's never rained since. I just wanted to settle in my mind whether or not that damn roof leaked."

So I quit Arizona, and in about a week I see my reflection in the winders of a little place called Cyanide in the Colorado mountains.

Fellows, she was a bird. They wasn't a pony in sight, nor a squar' foot of land that wasn't either street or straight up. It made me plumb lonesome for a country where you could see a long ways even if you didn't see much. And this early in the evenin' they wasn't hardly anybody in the streets at all.

I took a look at them dark, gloomy, old mountains, and a sniff at a breeze that would have frozen the whiskers of hope, and I made a dive for the nearest lit winder. They was a sign over it that just said:

THIS IS A SALOON

I was glad they labelled her. I'd never have known it. They had a fifteen-year old kid tendin' bar, no games goin', and not a soul in the place.

"Sorry to disturb your repose, bub," says I, "but see if you can sort out any rye among them collections of sassapariller of yours."

I took a drink, and then another to keep it company —I was beginnin' to sympathise with anythin' lonesome. Then I kind of sauntered out to the back room where the hurdy-gurdy ought to be. Sure enough, there was a girl settin' on the pianner stool, another in a chair, and a nice shiny Jew drummer danglin' his feet from a table. They looked up when they see me come in, and went right on talkin'.

"Hello, girls!" says I.

At that they stopped talkin' complete.

"How's tricks?" says I.

"Who's your woolly friend?" the shiny Jew asks of the girls.

I looked at him a minute, but I see he'd been raised

a pet, and then, too, I was so hungry for sassiety I was willin' to pass a bet or two.

"Don't you *admire* these cow gents?" snickers one of the girls.

"Play somethin', sister," says I to the one at the pianner.

She just grinned at me.

"Interdooce me," says the drummer in a kind of a way that made them all laugh a heap.

"Give us a tune," I begs, tryin' to be jolly, too.

"She don't know any pieces," says the Jew.

"Don't you?" I asks pretty sharp.

"No," says she.

"Well, I do," says I.

I walked up to her, jerked out my guns, and reached around both sides of her to the pianner. I run the muzzles up and down the keyboard two or three times, and then shot out half a dozen keys.

"That's the piece I know," says I.

But the other girl and the Jew drummer had punched the breeze.

The girl at the pianner just grinned, and pointed to the winder where they was some ragged glass hangin'. She was dead game.

"Say, Susie," says I, "you're all right, but your friends is tur'ble. I may be rough, and I ain't never been curried below the knees, but I'm better to tie to than them sons of guns."

"I believe it," says she.

So we had a drink at the bar, and started out to investigate the wonders of Cyanide.

Say, that night *was* a wonder. Susie faded after about three drinks, but I didn't seem to mind that. I hooked up to another saloon kept by a thin Dutchman. A fat Dutchman is stupid, but a thin one is all right.

In ten minutes I had more friends in Cyanide than they is fiddlers in hell. I begun to conclude Cyanide wasn't so lonesome. About four o'clock in comes a little Irishman about four foot high, with more upper lip than a muley cow, and enough red hair to make an artificial aurorer borealis. He had big red hands with freckles pasted onto them, and stiff red hairs standin' up separate and lonesome like signal stations. Also his legs was bowed.

He gets a drink at the bar, and stands back and yells:

"God bless the Irish and let the Dutch rustle!"

Now, this was none of my town, so I just stepped back of the end of the bar quick where I wouldn't stop no lead. The shootin' didn't begin.

"Probably Dutchy didn't take no note of what the locoed little dogie *did* say," thinks I to myself.

The Irishman bellied up to the bar again, and pounded on it with his fist.

"Look here!" he yells. "Listen to what I'm tellin' ye! God bless the Irish and let the Dutch rustle! Do ye hear me?"

"Sure, I hear ye," says Dutchy, and goes on swabbin' his bar with a towel.

At that my soul just grew sick. I asked the man next to me why Dutchy didn't kill the little fellow.

"Kill him!" says this man. "What for?"

"For insultin' of him, of course."

"Oh, he's drunk," says the man, as if that explained anythin'.

That settled it with me. I left that place, and went home, and it wasn't more than four o'clock, neither. No, I don't call four o'clock late. It may be a little late for night before last, but it's just the shank of the evenin' for to-night.

Well, it took me six weeks and two days to go

broke. I didn't know sic em' about minin'; and before long I *knew* that I didn't know sic 'em. Most all
day I poked around them mountains—not like our'n
—too much timber to be comfortable. At night I
got to droppin' in at Dutchy's. He had a couple
of quiet games goin', and they was one fellow among
that lot of grubbin' prairie dogs that had heerd tell
that cows had horns. He was the wisest of the bunch
on the cattle business. So I stowed away my conso-
lation, and made out to forget comparing Colorado
with God's country.

About three times a week this Irishman I told you
of—name O'Toole—comes bulgin' in. When he was
sober he talked minin' high, wide, and handsome.
When he was drunk he pounded both fists on the bar
and yelled for action, tryin' to get Dutchy on the
peck.

" God bless the Irish and let the Dutch rustle!"
he yells about six times. " Say, do you hear? "

" Sure," says Dutchy, calm as a milk cow, " sure,
I hears ye!"

I was plumb sorry for O'Toole. I'd like to have
given him a run; but, of course, I couldn't take it
up without makin' myself out a friend of this Dutchy

party, and I couldn't stand for that. But I did tackle Dutchy about it one night when they wasn't nobody else there.

" Dutchy," says I, " what makes you let that bow-legged cross between a bulldog and a flamin' red sunset tromp on you so? It looks to me like you're plumb spiritless."

Dutchy stopped wipin' glasses for a minute.

" Just you hold on," says he. " I ain't ready yet. Bimeby I make him sick; also those others who laugh with him."

He had a little grey flicker in his eye, and I thinks to myself that maybe they'd get Dutchy on the peck yet.

As I said, I went broke in just six weeks and two days. And I was broke a plenty. No hold-outs anywhere. It was a heap long ways to cows; and I'd be teetotally chawed up and spit out if I was goin' to join these minin' terrapins defacin' the bosom of nature. It sure looked to me like hard work.

While I was figurin' what next, Dutchy came in. Which I was tur'ble surprised at that, but I said good-mornin' and would he rest his poor feet.

" You like to make some money? " he asks.

"That depends," says I, "on how easy it is."

"It is easy," says he. "I want you to buy hosses for me."

"Hosses! Sure!" I yells, jumpin' up. "You bet you! Why, hosses is where I live! What hosses do you want?"

"All hosses," says he, calm as a faro dealer.

"What?" says I. "Elucidate, my bucko. I don't take no such blanket order. Spread your cards."

"I mean just that," says he. "I want you to buy all the hosses in this camp, and in the mountains. Every one."

"Whew!" I whistles. "That's a large order. But I'm your meat."

"Come with me, then," says he. I hadn't but just got up, but I went with him to his little old poison factory. Of course, I hadn't had no breakfast; but he staked me to a Kentucky breakfast. What's a Kentucky breakfast? Why, a Kentucky breakfast is a three-pound steak, a bottle of whisky, and a setter dog. What's the dog for? Why, to eat the steak, of course.

We come to an agreement. I was to get two-fifty a head commission. So I started out. There wasn't many hosses in that country, and what there was the owners hadn't much use for unless it was to work a whim. I picked up about a hundred head quick enough, and reported to Dutchy.

"How about burros and mules?" I asks Dutchy.

"They goes," says he. "Mules same as hosses; burros four bits a head to you."

At the end of a week I had a remuda of probably two hundred animals. We kept them over the hills in some "parks," as these sots call meadows in that country. I rode into town and told Dutchy.

"Got them all?" he asks.

"All but a cross-eyed buckskin that's mean, and the bay mare that Noah bred to."

"Get them," says he.

"The bandits want too much," I explains.

"Get them anyway," says he.

I went away and got them. It was scand'lous; such prices.

When I hit Cyanide again I ran into scenes of wild excitement. The whole passel of them was on that one street of their'n, talkin' sixteen ounces to the pound. In the middle was Dutchy, drunk as a soldier—just plain foolish drunk.

"Good Lord!" thinks I to myself, "he ain't celebratin' gettin' that bunch of buzzards, is he?"

But I found he wasn't that bad. When he caught sight of me, he fell on me drivellin'.

"Look there!" he weeps, showin' me a letter.

I was the last to come in; so I kept that letter— here she is. I'll read her.

DEAR DUTCHY:—I suppose you thought I'd flew the coop, but I haven't and this is to prove it. Pack up your outfit and hit the trail. I've made the biggest free gold strike you ever see. I'm sending you specimens. There's tons just like it, tons and tons. I got all the claims I can hold myself; but there's heaps more. I've writ to Johnny and Ed at Denver to come on. Don't give this away. Make tracks. Come in to Buck Cañon in the Whetstones and oblige.

Yours truly,

HENRY SMITH.

Somebody showed me a handful of white rock with yeller streaks in it. His eyes was bulgin' until you could have hung your hat on them. That O'Toole party was walkin' around, wettin' his lips with his tongue and swearin' soft.

"God bless the Irish and let the Dutch rustle!"

says he. "And the fool had to get drunk and give it away!"

The excitement was just started, but it didn't last long. The crowd got the same notion at the same time, and it just melted. Me and Dutchy was left alone.

I went home. Pretty soon a fellow named Jimmy Tack come around a little out of breath.

"Say, you know that buckskin you bought off'n me?" says he, "I want to buy him back."

"Oh, you do," says I.

"Yes," says he. "I've got to leave town for a couple of days, and I got to have somethin' to pack."

"Wait and I'll see," says I.

Outside the door I met another fellow.

"Look here," he stops me with. "How about that pay mare I sold you? Can you call that sale off? I got to leave town for a day or two and—— "

"Wait," says I. "I'll see."

By the gate was another hurryin' up.

"Oh, yes," says I when he opens his mouth. "I know all your troubles. You have to leave town for a couple of days, and you want back that lizard you sold me. Well, wait."

After that I had to quit the main street and dodge back of the hog ranch. They was all headed my way. I was as popular as a snake in a prohibition town.

I hit Dutchy's by the back door.

"Do you want to sell hosses?" I asks. "Everyone in town wants to buy."

Dutchy looked hurt.

"I wanted to keep them for the valley market," says he, "but—— How much did you give Jimmy Tack for his buckskin?"

"Twenty," says I.

"Well, let him have it for eighty," says Dutchy; "and the others in proportion."

I lay back and breathed hard.

"Sell them all, but the one best hoss," says he— "no, the *two* best."

"Holy smoke!" says I, gettin' my breath. "If you mean that, Dutchy, you lend me another gun and give me a drink."

He done so, and I went back home to where the whole camp of Cyanide was waitin'.

I got up and made them a speech and told them I'd sell them hosses all right, and to come back. Then

I got an Injin boy to help, and we rustled over the remuda and held them in a blind cañon. Then I called up these miners one at a time, and made bargains with them. Roar! Well, you could hear them at Denver, they tell me, and the weather reports said, " Thunder in the mountains." But it was cash on delivery, and they all paid up. They had seen that white quartz with the gold stickin' into it, and that's the same as a dose of loco to miner gents.

Why didn't I take a hoss and start first? I did think of it—for about one second. I wouldn't stay in that country then for a million dollars a minute. I was plumb sick and loathin' it, and just waitin' to make high jumps back to Arizona. So I wasn't aimin' to join this stampede, and didn't have no vivid emotions.

They got to fightin' on which should get the first hoss ; so I bent my gun on them and made them draw. lots. They roared some more, but done so ; and as fast as each one handed over his dust or dinero he made a rush for his cabin, piled on his saddle and pack, and pulled his freight in a cloud of dust. It was sure a grand stampede, and I enjoyed it no limit.

So by sundown I was alone with the Injin. Those two hundred head brought in about twenty thousand dollars. It was heavy, but I could carry it. I was about alone in the landscape; and there were the two best hosses I had saved out for Dutchy. I was sure some tempted. But I had enough to get home on anyway; and I never yet drank behind the bar, even if I might hold up the saloon from the floor. So I grieved some inside that I was so tur'ble conscientious, shouldered the sacks, and went down to find Dutchy.

I met him headed his way, and carryin' of a sheet of paper.

"Here's your dinero," says I, dumpin' the four big sacks on the ground.

He stooped over and hefted them. Then he passed one over to me.

"What's that for?" I asks.

"For you," says he.

"My commission ain't that much," I objects.

"You've earned it," says he, "and you might have skipped with the whole wad."

"How did you know I wouldn't?" I asks.

"Well," says he, and I noted that jag of his had

They got to fighten on which should get the first hoss; so I bent my gun on them and made them draw lots

flew. "You see, I was behind that rock up there, and I had you covered."

I saw; and I began to feel better about bein' so tur'ble conscientious.

We walked a little ways without sayin' nothin'.

"But ain't you goin' to join the game?" I asks.

"Guess not," says he, jinglin' of his gold. "I'm satisfied."

"But if you don't get a wiggle on you, you are sure goin' to get left on those gold claims," says I.

"There ain't no gold claims," says he.

"But Henry Smith——" I cries.

"There ain't no Henry Smith," says he.

I let that soak in about six inches.

"But there's a Buck Cañon," I pleads. "Please say there's a Buck Cañon."

"Oh, yes, there's a Buck Cañon," he allows. "Nice limestone formation—make good hard water."

"Well, you're a marvel," says I.

We walked on together down to Dutchy's saloon. We stopped outside.

"Now," says he, "I'm goin' to take one of those hosses and go somewheres else. Maybe you'd better do likewise on the other."

" You bet I will," says I.

He turned around and tacked up the paper he was carryin'. It was a sign. It read:

THE DUTCH HAS RUSTLED

" Nice sentiment," says I. " It will be appreciated when the crowd comes back from that little *pasear* into Buck Cañon. But why not tack her up where the trail hits the camp? Why on this particular door? "

" Well," said Dutchy, squintin' at the sign sideways, " you see I sold this place day before yesterday—to Mike O'Toole."

CHAPTER EIGHT

THE CORRAL BRANDING

ALL that night we slept like sticks of wood. No dreams visited us, but in accordance with the immemorial habit of those who live out—whether in the woods, on the plains, among the mountains, or at sea—once during the night each of us rose on his elbow, looked about him, and dropped back to sleep. If there had been a fire to replenish, that would have been the moment to do so; if the wind had been changing and the seas rising, that would have been the time to cast an eye aloft for indications, to feel whether the anchor cable was holding; if the pack-horses had straggled from the alpine meadows under the snows, this would have been the occasion for intent listening for the faintly tinkling bell so that next day one would know in which direction to look. But since there existed for us no responsibility, we each reported dutifully at the roll-call of habit, and dropped back into our blankets with a grateful sigh.

I remember the moon sailing a good gait among

apparently stationary cloudlets; I recall a deep, black shadow lying before distant silvery mountains; I glanced over the stark, motionless canvases, each of which concealed a man; the air trembled with the bellowing of cattle in the corrals.

Seemingly but a moment later the cook's howl brought me to consciousness again. A clear, licking little fire danced in the blackness. Before it moved silhouettes of men already eating.

I piled out and joined the group. Homer was busy distributing his men for the day. Three were to care for the remuda; five were to move the stray-herd from the corrals to good feed; three branding crews were told to brand the calves we had collected in the cut of the afternoon before. That took up about half the men. The rest were to make a short drive in the salt grass. I joined the Cattleman, and together we made our way afoot to the branding pen.

We were the only ones who did go afoot, however, although the corrals were not more than two hundred yards' distant. When we arrived we found the string of ponies standing around outside. Between the upright bars of greasewood we could see the cattle, and near the opposite side the men building a fire next the fence. We pushed open the wide gate and entered. The three ropers sat their horses, idly swinging the loops of their ropes back and forth. Three others brought wood and arranged it craftily in such manner as to get best draught for heating— a good branding fire is most decidedly a work of art. One stood waiting for them to finish, a sheaf of long J H stamping irons in his hand. All the rest squatted on their heels along the fence, smoking cigarettes and chatting together. The first rays of the sun slanted across in one great sweep from the remote mountains.

In ten minutes Charley pronounced the irons ready. Homer, Wooden, and old California John rode in among the cattle. The rest of the men arose and stretched their legs and advanced. The Cattleman and I climbed to the top bar of the gate, where we roosted, he with his tally-book on his knee.

Each rider swung his rope above his head with one hand, keeping the broad loop open by a skilful turn of the wrist at the end of each revolution. In a moment Homer leaned forward and threw. As the loop settled, he jerked sharply upward, exactly as one would strike to hook a big fish. This tightened the loop and prevented it from slipping off. Immediately, and without waiting to ascertain the result of the manœuvre, the horse turned and began methodically, without undue haste, to walk toward the branding fire. Homer wrapped the rope twice or thrice about the horn, and sat over in one stirrup to avoid the tightened line and to preserve the balance. Nobody paid any attention to the calf.

The latter had been caught by the two hind legs. As the rope tightened, he was suddenly upset, and before he could realise that something disagreeable was happening, he was sliding majestically along on his belly. Behind him followed his anxious mother, her head swinging from side to side.

Near the fire the horse stopped. The two "bulldoggers" immediately pounced upon the victim. It was promptly flopped over on its right side. One knelt on its head and twisted back its foreleg in a sort of hammer-lock; the other seized one hind foot, pressed his boot heel against the other hind leg close to the body, and sat down behind the animal. Thus the calf was unable to struggle. When once you have had the wind knocked out of you, or a rib or two broken, you cease to think this unnecessarily rough. Then one or the other threw off the rope. Homer rode away, coiling the rope as he went.

"Hot iron!" yelled one of the bull-doggers.

"Marker!" yelled the other.

Immediately two men ran forward. The brander pressed the iron smoothly against the flank. A smoke and the smell of scorching hair arose. Perhaps the calf blatted a little as the heat scorched. In a brief moment it was over. The brand showed cherry, which is the proper colour to indicate due peeling and a successful mark.

In the meantime the marker was engaged in his work. First, with a sharp knife he cut off slanting the upper quarter of one ear. Then he nicked out a swallow-tail in the other. The pieces he thrust into his pocket in order that at the completion of the work he could thus check the Cattleman's tally-board as to the number of calves branded.[1] The bull-dogger let go. The calf sprang up, was appropriated and smelled over by his worried mother, and the two departed into the herd to talk it over.

[1] For the benefit of the squeamish it might be well to state that the fragments of the ears were cartilaginous, and therefore not bloody.

It seems to me that a great deal of unnecessary twaddle is abroad as to the extreme cruelty of branding. Undoubtedly it is to some extent painful, and could some other method of ready identification be devised, it might be as well to adopt it in preference. But in the circumstance of a free range, thousands of cattle, and hundreds of owners, any other method is out of the question. I remember a New England movement looking toward small brass tags to be hung from the ear. Inextinguishable laughter followed the spread of this doctrine through Arizona. Imagine a puncher descending to examine politely the ear-tags of wild cattle on the open range or in a round-up.

But, as I have intimated, even the inevitable branding and ear-marking are not so painful as one might suppose. The scorching hardly penetrates below the outer tough skin—only enough to kill the roots of the hair—besides which it must be remembered that cattle are not so sensitive as the higher nervous organisms. A calf usually bellows when the iron bites, but as soon as released he almost invariably goes to feeding or to looking idly about. Indeed, I have never seen one even take the trouble to lick his wounds, which is certainly not true in the case of the injuries they inflict on each other in fighting. Besides which, it happens but once in a lifetime, and is over in ten seconds; a comfort denied to those of us who have our teeth filled.

In the meantime two other calves had been roped by the two other men. One of the little animals was but a few months old, so the rider did not bother with its hind legs, but tossed his loop over its neck. Naturally, when things tightened up, Mr. Calf entered his objections, which took the form of most vigorous bawlings, and the most comical bucking, pitching, cavorting, and bounding in the air. Mr. Frost's bull-calf alone in pictorial history shows the attitudes. And then, of course, there was the gorgeous contrast between all this frantic and uncomprehending excitement and the absolute matter-of-fact imperturbability of horse and rider. Once at the fire, one of the men seized the tightened rope in one hand, reached well over the animal's back to get a slack of the loose hide next the belly, lifted strongly, and tripped. This is called "bull-dogging." As he knew his business, and as the calf was a small one, the little beast went over promptly, hit the ground with a whack, and was pounced upon and held.

Such good luck did not always follow, however. An occasional and exceedingly husky bull yearling declined to be upset in any such manner. He would catch himself on one foot, scramble vigorously, and end by struggling back to the upright. Then ten to one he made a dash to get away. In such case he was generally snubbed up short enough at the end of the rope; but once or twice he succeeded in running around a group absorbed in branding. You can imagine what happened next. The rope, attached at one end to a conscientious and immovable horse and at the other to a reckless and vigorous little bull, swept its taut and destroying way about mid-knee high across that group. The brander and marker, who were standing, promptly sat down hard; the bull-doggers, who were sitting, immediately turned several most capable somersaults; the other calf arose and inextricably entangled his rope with that of his accomplice. Hot irons, hot language, and dust filled the air.

Another method, and one requiring slightly more knack, is to grasp the animal's tail and throw it by a quick jerk across the pressure of the rope. This is productive of some fun if it fails.

By now the branding was in full swing. The three horses came and went phlegmatically. When the nooses fell, they turned and walked toward the fire as a matter of course. Rarely did the cast fail. Men ran to and fro busy and intent. Sometimes three or four calves were on the ground at once. Cries arose in a confusion: "Marker!" "Hot iron!" "Tally one!" Dust eddied and dissipated. Behind all were clear sunlight and the organ roll of the cattle bellowing.

Toward the middle of the morning the bull-doggers began to get a little tired.

"No more necked calves," they announced. "Catch 'em by the hind legs, or bull-dog 'em yourself."

And that went. Once in a while the rider, lazy, or careless, or bothered by the press of numbers, dragged up a victim caught by the neck. The bull-doggers flatly refused to have anything to do with it. An obvious way out would have been to flip off the loop and try again; but of course that would have amounted to a confession of wrong.

"You fellows drive me plumb weary," remarked the rider, slowly dismounting. "A little bit of a calf like that! What you all need is a nigger to cut up your food for you!"

Then he would spit on his hands and go at it alone. If luck attended his first effort, his sarcasm was profound.

"There's yore little calf," said he. "Would you like to have me tote it to you, or do you reckon you could toddle this far with yore little old iron?"

But if the calf gave much trouble, then all work ceased while the unfortunate puncher wrestled it down.

Toward noon the work slacked. Unbranded calves were scarce. Sometimes the men rode here and there for a minute or so before their eyes fell on a pair of uncropped ears. Finally Homer rode over to the Cattleman and reported the branding finished. The latter counted the marks in his tally-book.

"One hundred and seventy-six," he announced.

The markers, squatted on their heels, told over the bits of ears they had saved. The total amounted to but an hundred and seventy-five. Everybody went to searching for the missing bit. It was not forthcoming. Finally Wooden discovered it in his hip pocket.

" Felt her thar all the time," said he, " but thought it must shorely be a chaw of tobacco."

This matter satisfactorily adjusted, the men all ran for their ponies. They had been doing a wrestler's heavy work all the morning, but did not seem to be tired. I saw once in some crank physical culture periodical that a cowboy's life was physically ill-balanced, like an oarsman's, in that it exercised only certain muscles of the body. The writer should be turned loose in a branding corral.

Through the wide gates the cattle were urged out to the open plain. There they were held for over an hour while the cows wandered about looking for their lost progeny. A cow knows her calf by scent and sound, not by sight. Therefore the noise was deafening, and the motion incessant.

Finally the last and most foolish cow found the last and most foolish calf. We turned the herd loose to hunt water and grass at its own pleasure, and went slowly back to chuck.

CHAPTER NINE

THE OLD TIMER

ABOUT a week later, in the course of the round-up, we reached the valley of the Box Springs, where we camped for some days at the dilapidated and abandoned adobe structure that had once been a ranch house of some importance.

Just at dusk one afternoon we finished cutting the herd which our morning's drive had collected. The stray-herd, with its new additions from the day's work, we pushed rapidly into one big stock corral. The cows and unbranded calves we urged into another. Fifty head of beef steers found asylum from dust, heat, and racing to and fro, in the mile square wire enclosure called the pasture. All the remainder, for which we had no further use we drove out of the flat into the brush and toward the distant mountains. Then we let them go as best pleased them.

By now the desert had turned slate-coloured, and the brush was olive green with evening. The hard, uncompromising ranges, twenty miles to eastward, had softened behind a wonderful veil of purple and pink, vivid as the chiffon of a girl's gown. To the south and southwest the Chiricahuas and Dragoons were lost in thunderclouds which flashed and rumbled.

We jogged homewards, our cutting ponies, tired with the quick, sharp work, shuffling knee deep in a dusk that seemed to disengage itself and rise upwards from the surface of the desert. Everybody was hungry and tired. At the chuck wagon we threw off our saddles and turned the mounts into the remuda. Some of the wisest of us, remembering the thunderclouds, stacked our gear under the veranda roof of the old ranch house.

Supper was ready. We seized the tin battery, filled the plates with the meat, bread, and canned corn, and squatted on our heels. The food was good, and we ate hugely in silence. When we could hold no more we lit pipes. Then we had leisure to notice that the storm cloud was mounting in a portentous silence to the zenith, quenching the brilliant desert, stars.

"Rolls" were scattered everywhere. A roll includes a cowboy's bed and all of his personal belongings. When the outfit includes a bed-wagon, the roll assumes bulky proportions.

As soon as we had come to a definite conclusion that it was going to rain, we deserted the camp fire and went rustling for our blankets. At the end of ten minutes every bed was safe within the doors of the abandoned adobe ranch house, each owner recumbent on the floor claim he had pre-empted, and every man hoping fervently that he had guessed right as to the location of leaks.

Ordinarily we had depended on the light of camp fires, so now artificial illumination lacked. Each man was indicated by the alternately glowing and waning lozenge of his cigarette fire. Occasionally someone struck a match, revealing for a moment high-lights on bronzed countenances, and the silhouette of a shading hand. Voices spoke disembodied. As the conversation developed, we gradually recognised the membership of our own roomful. I had forgotten to state that the ranch house included four chambers. Outside, the rain roared with Arizona ferocity. Inside, men congratulated themselves, or swore as leaks developed and localised.

Naturally we talked first of stampedes. Cows and

bears are the two great cattle-country topics. Then we had a mouth-organ solo or two, which naturally led on to songs. My turn came. I struck up the first verse of a sailor chantey as possessing at least the interest of novelty:

Oh, once we were a-sailing, a-sailing were we,
Blow high, blow low, what care we;
And we were a-sailing to see what we could see,
Down on the coast of the High Barbaree.

I had just gone so far when I was brought up short by a tremendous oath behind me. At the same instant a match flared. I turned to face a stranger holding the little light above his head, and peering with fiery intentness over the group sprawled about the floor.

He was evidently just in from the storm. His dripping hat lay at his feet. A shock of straight, close-clipped vigorous hair stood up grey above his seamed forehead. Bushy iron-grey eyebrows drawn close together thatched a pair of burning, unquenchable eyes. A square, deep jaw, lightly stubbled with grey, was clamped so tight that the cheek muscles above it stood out in knots and welts.

Then the match burned his thick, square fingers,

and he dropped it into the darkness that ascended to swallow it.

"Who was singing that song?" he cried harshly. Nobody answered.

"Who was that singing?" he demanded again.

By this time I had recovered from my first astonishment.

"I was singing," said I.

Another match was instantly lit and thrust into my very face. I underwent the fierce scrutiny of an instant, then the taper was thrown away half consumed.

"Where did you learn it?" the stranger asked in an altered voice.

"I don't remember," I replied; "it is a common enough deep-sea chantey."

A heavy pause fell. Finally the stranger sighed.

"Quite like," he said; "I never heard but one man sing it."

"Who in hell are you?" someone demanded out of the darkness.

Before replying, the newcomer lit a third match, searching for a place to sit down. As he bent forward, his strong, harsh face once more came clearly into view.

" He's Colorado Rogers," the Cattleman answered for him; " I know him."

" Well," insisted the first voice, " what in hell does Colorado Rogers mean by bustin' in on our song *fiesta* that way? "

" Tell them, Rogers," advised the Cattleman, " tell them—just as you told it down on the Gila ten years ago next month."

" What? " inquired Rogers. " Who are you? "

" You don't know me," replied the Cattleman, " but I was with Buck Johnson's outfit then. Give us the yarn."

" Well," agreed Rogers, " pass over the ' makings ' and I will."

He rolled and lit a cigarette, while I revelled in the memory of his rich, great voice. It was of the sort made to declaim against the sea or the rush of rivers or, as here, the fall of waters and the thunder—full, from the chest, with the caressing throat vibration that gives colour to the most ordinary statements. After ten words we sank back oblivious of the storm, forgetful of the leaky roof and the dirty floor, lost in the story told us by the Old Timer.

CHAPTER TEN

THE TEXAS RANGERS

I CAME from Texas, like the bulk of you punchers, but a good while before the most of you were born. That was forty-odd years ago—and I've been on the Colorado River ever since. That's why they call me Colorado Rogers. About a dozen of us came out together. We had all been Texas Rangers, but when the war broke out we were out of a job. We none of us cared much for the Johnny Rebs, and still less for the Yanks, so we struck overland for the West, with the idea of hitting the California diggings.

Well, we got switched off one way and another. When we got down to about where Douglas is now, we found that the Mexican Government was offering a bounty for Apache scalps. That looked pretty good to us, for Injin chasing was our job, so we started in to collect. Did pretty well, too, for about three months, and then the Injins began to get too scarce, or too plenty in streaks. Looked like our job was over with, but some of the boys discovered that Mexicans, having straight black hair, you couldn't tell one of their scalps from an Apache's. After that the bounty business picked up for a while. It was too much for me, though, and I quit the outfit and pushed on alone until I struck the Colorado about where Yuma is now.

At that time the California immigrants by the southern route used to cross just there, and these Yuma Injins had a monopoly on the ferry business. They were a peaceful, fine-looking lot, without a thing on but a gee-string. The women had belts with rawhide strings hanging to the knees. They put them on one over the other until they didn't feel too decollotey. It wasn't until the soldiers came that the officers' wives got them to wear handkerchiefs over their breasts. The system was all right, though. They wallowed around in the hot, clean sand, like chickens, and kept healthy. Since they took to wearing clothes they've been petering out, and dying of dirt and assorted diseases.

They ran this ferry monopoly by means of boats made of tules, charged a scand'lous low price, and everything was happy and lovely. I ran on a little bar and panned out some dust, so I camped a while, washing gold, getting friendly with the Yumas, and talking horse and other things with the immigrants.

About a month of this, and the Texas boys drifted in. Seems they sort of overdid the scalp matter, and got found out. When they saw me, they stopped and went into camp. They'd travelled a heap of desert, and were getting sick of it. For a while they tried gold washing, but I had the only pocket—and that was about skinned. One evening a fellow named Walleye announced that he had been doing some figuring, and wanted to make a speech. We told him to fire ahead.

" Now look here," said he, " what's the use of going to California? Why not stay here? "

" What in hell would we do here? " someone asked. " Collect Gila monsters for their good looks? "

" Don't get gay," said Walleye. " What's the matter with going into business? Here's a heap of people going through, and more coming every day. This ferry business could be made to pay big. Them Injins charges two bits a head. That's a crime for the only way across. And how much do you sup-

pose whisky'd be worth to drink after that desert?
And a man's so sick of himself by the time he gets
this far that he'd play chuck-a-luck, let alone faro
or monte."

That kind of talk hit them where they lived, and
Yuma was founded right then and there. They
hadn't any whisky yet, but cards were plenty, and
the ferry monopoly was too easy. Walleye served
notice on the Injins that a dollar a head went; and
we all set to building a tule raft like the others.
Then the wild bunch got uneasy, so they walked
upstream one morning and stole the Injins' boats.
The Injins came after them innocent as babies, thinking the raft had gone adrift. When they got into
camp our men opened up and killed four of them
as a kind of hint. After that the ferry company
didn't have any trouble. The Yumas moved up river
a ways, where they've lived ever since. They got
the corpses and buried them. That is, they dug a
trench for each one and laid poles across it, with
a funeral pyre on the poles. Then they put the body
on top, and the women of the family cut their
hair off and threw it on. After that they set fire
to the outfit, and, when the poles had burned through,

the whole business fell into the trench of its own accord. It was the neatest, automatic, self-cocking, double-action sort of a funeral I ever saw. There wasn't any ceremony—only crying.

The ferry business flourished at prices which were sometimes hard to collect. But it was a case of pay or go back, and it was a tur'ble long ways back. We got us timbers and made a scow; built a *baile* and saloon and houses out of adobe; and called her Yuma, after the Injins that had really started her. We got our supplies through the Gulf of California, where sailing boats worked up the river. People began to come in for one reason or another, and first thing we knew we had a store and all sorts of trimmings. In fact we was a real live town.

CHAPTER ELEVEN

THE SAILOR WITH ONE HAND

At this moment the heavy beat of the storm on the roof ceased with miraculous suddenness, leaving the outside world empty of sound save for the *drip, drip, drip* of eaves. Nobody ventured to fill in the pause that followed the stranger's last words, so in a moment he continued his narrative.

We had every sort of people with us off and on, and, as I was lookout at a popular game, I saw them all. One evening I was on my way home about two o'clock of a moonlit night, when on the edge of the shadow I stumbled over a body lying part across the footway. At the same instant I heard the rip of steel through cloth and felt a sharp stab in my left leg. For a minute I thought some drunk had used his knife on me, and I mighty near derringered him as he lay. But somehow I didn't, and looking closer, I saw the man was unconscious. Then I scouted to see what had cut me, and found that the fellow had lost a hand. In place of it he wore a sharp steel hook. This I had tangled up with and gotten well pricked.

I dragged him out into the light. He was a slim-built young fellow, with straight black hair, long and lank and oily, a lean face, and big hooked nose. He had on only a thin shirt, a pair of rough wool pants, and the rawhide home-made *zapatos* the Mexicans wore then instead of boots. Across his forehead ran a long gash, cutting his left eyebrow square in two.

There was no doubt of his being alive, for he was breathing hard, like a man does when he gets hit over the head. It didn't sound good. When a man breathes that way he's mostly all gone.

Well, it was really none of my business, as you might say. Men got batted over the head often enough in those days. But for some reason I picked him up and carried him to my 'dobe shack, and laid him out, and washed his cut with sour wine. That brought him to. Sour wine is fine to put a wound in shape to heal, but it's no soothing syrup. He sat up as though he'd been touched with a hot poker,

stared around wild-eyed, and cut loose with that
song you were singing. Only it wasn't that verse.
It was another one further along, that went like this:

> Their coffin was their ship, and their grave it was the
> sea,
> *Blow high, blow low, what care we;*
> And the quarter that we gave them was to sink them in
> the sea,
> *Down on the coast of the High Barbaree.*

It fair made my hair rise to hear him, with the
big, still, solemn desert outside, and the quiet moon-
lignt, and the shadows, and him sitting up straight
and gaunt, his eyes blazing each side his big eagle
nose, and his snaky hair hanging over the raw cut
across his head. However, I made out to get him
bandaged up and in shape; and pretty soon he sort
of went to sleep.

Well, he was clean out of his head for nigh two
weeks. Most of the time he lay flat on his back
staring at the pole roof, his eyes burning and looking like they saw each one something a different distance off, the way crazy eyes do. That was when he
was best. Then again he'd sing that Barbaree song
until I'd go out and look at the old Colorado flowing

by just to be sure I hadn't died and gone below. Or else he'd just talk. That was the worst perform- ance of all. It was like listening to one end of a telephone, though we didn't know what telephones were in those days. He began when he was a kid, and he gave his side of conversations, pausing for replies. I could mighty near furnish the replies sometimes. It was queer lingo—about ships and ships' officers and gales and calms and fights and pearls and whales and islands and birds and skies. But it was all little stuff. I used to listen by the hour, but I never made out anything really important as to who the man was, or where he'd come from, or what he'd done.

At the end of the second week I came in at noon as per usual to fix him up with grub. I didn't pay any attention to him, for he was quiet. As I was bending over the fire he spoke. Usually I didn't bother with his talk, for it didn't mean anything, but something in his voice made me turn. He was lying on his side, those black eyes of his blazing at me, but now both of them saw the same distance.

"Where are my clothes?" he asked, very in- tense.

"You ain't in any shape to want clothes," said I. "Lie still."

I hadn't any more than got the words out of my mouth before he was atop me. His method was a winner. He had me by the throat with his hand, and I felt the point of the hook pricking the back of my neck. One little squeeze—— Talk about your deadly weapons!

But he'd been too sick and too long abed. He turned dizzy and keeled over, and I dumped him back on the bunk. Then I put my six-shooter on.

In a minute or so he came to.

"Now you're a nice, sweet proposition," said I, as soon as I was sure he could understand me. "Here I pick you up on the street and save your worthless carcass, and the first chance you get you try to crawl my hump. Explain."

"Where's my clothes?" he demanded again, very fierce.

"For heaven's sake," I yelled at him, "what's the matter with you and your old clothes? There ain't enough of them to dust a fiddle with anyway. What do you think I'd want with them? They're safe enough."

"Let me have them," he begged.

"Now, look here," said I, "you can't get up to-day. You ain't fit."

"I know," he pleaded, "but let me see them."

Just to satisfy him I passed over his old duds.

"I've been robbed," he cried.

"Well," said I, "what did you expect would happen to you lying around Yuma after midnight with a hole in your head?"

"Where's my coat?" he asked.

"You had no coat when I picked you up," I replied.

He looked at me mighty suspicious, but didn't say anything more—wouldn't even answer when I spoke to him. After he'd eaten a fair meal he fell asleep. When I came back that evening the bunk was empty and he was gone.

I didn't see him again for two days. Then I caught sight of him quite a ways off. He nodded at me very sour, and dodged around the corner of the store.

"Guess he suspicions I stole that old coat of his," thinks I; and afterwards I found that my surmise had been correct.

SAILOR WITH ONE HAND 173

However, he didn't stay long in that frame of
mind. It was along towards evening, and I was
walking on the banks looking down over the muddy
old Colorado, as I always liked to do. The sun had
just set, and the mountains had turned hard and stiff,
as they do after the glow, and the sky above them
was a thousand million miles deep of pale green-
gold light. A pair of Greasers were ahead of me,
but I could see only their outlines, and they didn't
seem to interfere any with the scenery. Suddenly
a black figure seemed to rise up out of the ground;
the Mexican man went down as though he'd been
jerked with a string, and the woman screeched.

I ran up, pulling my gun. The Mex was flat on
his face, his arms stretched out. On the middle of
his back knelt my one-armed friend. And that sharp
hook was caught neatly under the point of the Mexican's jaw. You bet he lay still.

I really think I was just in time to save the man's
life. According to my belief another minute would
have buried the hook in the Mexican's neck. Anyway,
I thrust the muzzle of my Colt's into the sailor's
face.

" What's this? " I asked.

The sailor looked up at me without changing his position. He was not the least bit afraid.

" This man has my coat," he explained.

" Where'd you get the coat? " I asked the Mex.

" I ween heem at monte off Antonio Curvez," said he.

" Maybe," growled the sailor.

He still held the hook under the man's jaw, but with the other hand he ran rapidly under and over the Mexican's left shoulder. In the half light I could see his face change. The gleam died from his eye; the snarl left his lips. Without further delay he arose to his feet.

" Get up and give it here," he demanded.

The Mexican was only too glad to get off so easy. I don't know whether he'd really won the coat at monte or not. In any case, he flew *poco pronto*, leaving me and my friend together.

The man with the hook felt the left shoulder of the coat again, looked up, met my eye, muttered something intended to be pleasant, and walked away.

This was in December.

During the next two months he was a good deal about town, mostly doing odd jobs. I saw him off and on. He always spoke to me as pleasantly as he knew how, and once made some sort of a bluff about paying me back for my trouble in bringing him around. However, I didn't pay much attention to that, being at the time almighty busy holding down my card games.

The last day of February I was sitting in my shack smoking a pipe after supper, when my one-armed friend opened the door a foot, slipped in, and shut it immediately. By the time he looked towards me I knew where my six-shooter was.

" That's all right," said I, " but you better stay right there."

I intended to take no more chances with that hook.

He stood there looking straight at me without winking or offering to move.

" What do you want? " I asked.

" I want to make up to you for your trouble," said he. " I've got a good thing, and I want to let you in on it."

" What kind of a good thing? " I asked.

" Treasure," said he.

" H'm," said I.

I examined him closely. He looked all right enough, neither drunk nor loco.

" Sit down," said I—" over there; the other side the table." He did so. " Now, fire away," said I.

He told me his name was Solomon Anderson, but that he was generally known as Handy Solomon, on account of his hook; that he had always followed the sea; that lately he had coasted the west shores of Mexico; that at Guaymas he had fallen in with Spanish friends, in company with whom he had visited the mines in the Sierra Madre; that on this expedition the party had been attacked by Yaquis and wiped out, he alone surviving; that his blanket-mate before expiring had told him of gold buried in a cove of Lower California by the man's grandfather; that the man had given him a chart showing the location of the treasure; that he had sewn this chart in the shoulder of his coat, whence his suspicion of me and his being so loco about getting it back.

" And it's a big thing," said Handy Solomon to me, " for they's not only gold, but altar jewels and diamonds. It will make us rich, and a dozen like us, and you can kiss the Book on that."

" That may all be true," said I, " but why do you tell me? Why don't you get your treasure without the need of dividing it? "

" Why, mate," he answered, " it's just plain gratitude. Didn't you save my life, and nuss me, and take care of me when I was nigh killed? "

" Look here, Anderson, or Handy Solomon, or whatever you please to call yourself," I rejoined to this, " if you're going to do business with me—and I do not understand yet just what it is you want of me—you'll have to talk straight. It's all very well to say gratitude, but that don't go with me. You've been around here three months, and barring a half-dozen civil words and twice as many of the other kind, I've failed to see any indications of your gratitude before. It's a quality with a hell of a hang-fire to it."

He looked at me sideways, spat, and looked at me sideways again. Then he burst into a laugh.

" The devil's a preacher, if you ain't lost your pin-feathers," said he. " Well, it's this then: I got to have a boat to get there; and she must be stocked. And I got to have help with the treasure, if it's like this fellow said it was. And the Yaquis and can-

nibals from Tiburon is through the country. It's
money I got to have, and it's money I haven't got,
and can't get unless I let somebody in as pardner."

"Why me?" I asked.

"Why not?" he retorted. "I ain't see anybody
I like better."

We talked the matter over at length. I had to
force him to each point, for suspicion was strong
in him. I stood out for a larger party. He strongly
opposed this as depreciating the shares, but I had
no intention of going alone into what was then
considered a wild and dangerous country. Finally
we compromised. A third of the treasure was to go
to him, a third to me, and the rest was to be divided
among the men whom I should select. This scheme
did not appeal to him.

"How do I know you plays fair?" he complained.
"They'll be four of you to one of me; and I don't
like it, and you can kiss the Book on that."

"If you don't like it, leave it," said I, "and get
out, and be damned to you."

Finally he agreed; but he refused me a look at the
chart, saying that he had left it in a safe place. I
believe in reality he wanted to be surer of me, and
for that I can hardly blame him.

CHAPTER TWELVE

THE MURDER ON THE BEACH

AT this moment the cook stuck his head in at the open door.

"Say, you fellows," he complained, "I got to be up at three o'clock. Ain't you *never* goin' to turn in?"

"Shut up, Doctor!" "Somebody kill him!" "Here, sit down and listen to this yarn!" yelled a savage chorus.

There ensued a slight scuffle, a few objections. Then silence, and the stranger took up his story.

I had a chum named Billy Simpson, and I rung him in for friendship. Then there was a solemn, tall Texas young fellow, strong as a bull, straight and tough, brought up fighting Injins. He never said much, but I knew he'd be right there when the gong struck. For fourth man I picked out a German named Schwartz. He and Simpson had just come back from the mines together. I took him because he was a friend of Billy's, and besides was young and strong, and was the only man in town excepting the sailor, Anderson, who knew anything about running a boat. I forgot to say that the Texas fellow was named Denton.

Handy Solomon had his boat all picked out. It belonged to some Basques who had sailed her around from California. I must say when I saw her I felt inclined to renig, for she wasn't more'n about twenty-five feet long, was open except for a little sort of cubby-hole up in the front of her, had one mast, and was pointed at both ends. However, Schwartz said she was all right. He claimed he knew the kind; that she was the sort used by French fishermen, and could stand all sorts of trouble. She didn't look it.

We worked her up to Yuma, partly with oars and partly by sails. Then we loaded her with grub for a month. Each of us had his own weapons, of course. In addition we put in picks and shovels, and a small cask of water. Handy Solomon said that would be enough, as there was water marked down on his chart. We told t' e gang that we were going trading.

At the end of the week we started, and were out four days. There wasn't much room, what with the supplies and the baggage, for the five of us. We had to curl up 'most anywheres to sleep. And it certainly seemed to me that we were in lots of danger. The waves were much bigger than she was, and splashed on us considerable, but Schwartz and Anderson didn't seem to mind. They laughed at us. Anderson sang that song of his, and Schwartz told us of the placers he had worked. He and Simpson had made a pretty good clean-up, just enough to make them want to get rich. The first day out Simpson showed us a belt with about an hundred ounces of dust. This he got tired of wearing, so he kept it in a compass-box, which was empty.

At the end of the four days we turned in at a deep bay and came to anchor. The country was the usual proposition—very light-brown, brittle-looking mountains, about two thousand feet high; lots of sage and cactus, a pebbly beach, and not a sign of anything fresh and green.

But Denton and I were mighty glad to see any sort of land. Besides, our keg of water was pretty low, and it was getting about time to discover the spring the chart spoke of. So we piled our camp stuff in the small boat and rowed ashore.

Anderson led the way confidently enough up a
dry arroyo, whose sides were clay and conglomerate.
But, though we followed it to the end, we could find
no indications that it was anything more than a
wash for rain floods.

" That's main queer," muttered Anderson, and
returned to the beach.

There he spread out the chart—the first look at it
we'd had—and set to studying it.

It was a careful piece of work done in India ink,
pretty old, to judge by the look of it, and with all
sorts of pictures of mountains and dolphins and
ships and anchors around the edge. There was our
bay, all right. Two crosses were marked on the land
part—one labelled " *oro* " and the other " *agua*."

" Now there's the high cliff," says Anderson, following it out, " and there's the round hill with the
boulder—and if them bearings don't point due for
that ravine, the devil's a preacher."

We tried it again, with the same result. A second inspection of the map brought us no light on
the question. We talked it over, and looked at it
from all points, but we couldn't dodge the truth:
the chart was wrong.

Then we explored several of the nearest gullies, but without finding anything but loose stones baked hot in the sun.

By now it was getting towards sundown, so we built us a fire of mesquite on the beach, made us supper, and boiled a pot of beans.

We talked it over. The water was about gone.

"That's what we've got to find first," said Simpson, "no question of it. It's God knows how far to the next water, and we don't know how long it will take us to get there in that little boat. If we run our water entirely out before we start, we're going to be in trouble. We'll have a good look to-morrow, and if we don't find her, we'll run down to Mollyhay[1] and get a few extra casks."

"Perhaps that map is wrong about the treasure, too," suggested Denton.

"I thought of that," said Handy Solomon, "but then, thinks I to myself, this old rip probably don't make no long stay here—just dodges in and out like, between tides, to bury his loot. He would need no water at the time; but he might when he came back, so he marked the water on his map. But he

[1] Mulege—I retain the Old Timer's pronunciation.

wasn't noways particular *and* exact, being in a hurry. But you can kiss the Book to it that he didn't make no such mistakes about the swag."

" I believe you're right," said I.

When we came to turn in, Anderson suggested that he should sleep aboard the boat. But Billy Simpson, in mind perhaps of the hundred ounces in the compass-box, insisted that he'd just as soon as not. After a little objection Handy Solomon gave in, but I thought he seemed sour about it. We built a good fire, and in about ten seconds were asleep.

Now, usually I sleep like a log, and did this time until about midnight. Then all at once I came broad awake and sitting up in my blankets. Nothing had happened—I wasn't even dreaming—but there I was as alert and clear as though it were broad noon.

By the light of the fire I saw Handy Solomon sitting, and at his side our five rifles gathered.

I must have made some noise, for he turned quietly toward me, saw I was awake, and nodded. The moonlight was sparkling on the hard stony landscape, and a thin dampness came out from the sea.

After a minute Anderson threw on another stick of wood, yawned, and stood up.

" It's wet," said he; " I've been fixing the guns."

He showed me how he was inserting a little patch of felt between the hammer and the nipple—a scheme of his own for keeping damp from the powder. Then he rolled up in his blanket. At the time it all seemed quite natural—I suppose my mind wasn't fully awake, for all my head felt so clear. Afterwards I realised what a ridiculous bluff he was making: for of course the cap already on the nipple was plenty to keep out the damp. I fully believe he intended to kill us as we lay. Only my sudden awakening spoiled his plan.

I had absolutely no idea of this at the time, however. Not the slightest suspicion entered my head. In view of that fact, I have since believed in guardian angels. For my next move, which at the time seemed to me absolutely aimless, was to change my blankets from one side of the fire to the other. And that brought me alongside the five rifles.

Owing to this fact, I am now convinced, we awoke safe at daylight, cooked breakfast, and laid the plan for the day. Anderson directed us. I was to climb over the ridge before us and search in the ravine on the other side. Schwartz was to explore up the beach to the left, and Denton to the right. Anderson said he would wait for Billy Simpson, who had over-slept in the darkness of the cubby-hole, and who was now paddling ashore. The two of them would push inland to the west until a high hill would give them a chance to look around for greenery.

We started at once, before the sun would be hot. The hill I had to climb was steep and covered with *chollas,* so I didn't get along very fast. When I was about half way to the top I heard a shot from the beach. I looked back. Anderson was in the small boat, rowing rapidly out to the vessel. Denton was running up the beach from one direction and Schwartz from the other. I slid and slipped down the bluff, getting pretty well stuck up with the *cholla* spines.

At the beach we found Billy Simpson lying on his face, shot through the back. We turned him over, but he was apparently dead. Anderson had hoisted the sail, had cut loose from the anchor, and was sailing away.

Denton stood up straight and tall, looking. Then he pulled his belt in a hole, grabbed my arm, and started to run up the long curve of the beach. Behind us came Schwartz. We ran near a mile, and then fell among some tules in an inlet at the farther point.

"What is it?" I gasped.

"Our only chance—to get him——" said Denton. "He's got to go around this point—big wind— perhaps his mast will bust—then he'll come ashore——" He opened and shut his big brown hands.

So there we two fools lay, like panthers in the tules, taking our only one-in-a-million chance to lay hands on Anderson. Any sailor could have told us that the mast wouldn't break, but we had winded Schwartz a quarter of a mile back. And so we waited, our eyes fixed on the boat's sail, grudging her every inch, just burning to fix things to suit us a little better. And naturally she made the point in what I now know was only a fresh breeze, squared away, and dropped down before the wind toward Guaymas.

We walked back slowly to our camp, swallowing the copper taste of too hard a run. Schwartz we picked up from a boulder, just recovering. We were all of us crazy mad. Schwartz half wept, and blamed and cussed. Denton glowered away

in silence. I ground my feet into the sand in a helpless sort of anger, not only at the man himself, but
also at the whole way things had turned out. I don't
believe the least notion of our predicament had come
to any of us. All we knew yet was that we had
been done up, and we were hostile about it.

But at camp we found something to occupy us
for the moment. Poor Billy was not dead, as we had
supposed, but very weak and sick, and a hole square
through him. When we returned he was conscious,
but that was about all. His eyes were shut, and he
was moaning. I tore open his shirt to stanch the
blood. He felt my hand and opened his eyes. They
were glazed, and I don't think he saw me.

"Water, water!" he cried.

At that we others saw all at once where we stood.
I remember I rose to my feet and found myself
staring straight into Tom Denton's eyes. We looked
at each other that way for I guess it was a full
minute. Then Tom shook his head.

"Water, water!" begged poor Billy.

Tom leaned over him.

"My God, Billy, there ain't any water!" said he.

CHAPTER THIRTEEN

BURIED TREASURE

THE Old Timer's voice broke a little. We had leisure to notice that even the drip from the eaves had ceased. A faint, diffused light vouchsafed us dim outlines of sprawling figures and tumbled bedding. Far in the distance outside a wolf yelped.

We could do nothing for him except shelter him from the sun, and wet his forehead with sea-water; nor could we think clearly for ourselves as long as the spark of life lingered in him. His chest rose and fell regularly, but with long pauses between. When the sun was overhead he suddenly opened his eyes.

" Fellows," said he, " it's beautiful over there; the grass is so green, and the water so cool; I am tired of marching, and I reckon I'll cross over and camp."

Then he died. We scooped out a shallow hole above tide-mark, and laid him in it, and piled over him stones from the wash.

Then we went back to the beach, very solemn, to talk it over.

"Now, boys," said I, "there seems to me just one thing to do, and that is to pike out for water as fast as we can."

"Where?" asked Denton.

"Well," I argued, "I don't believe there's any water about this bay. Maybe there was when that chart was made. It was a long time ago. And anyway, the old pirate was a sailor, and no plainsman, and maybe he mistook rainwater for a spring. We've looked around this end of the bay. The chances are we'd use up two or three days exploring around the other, and then wouldn't be as well off as we are right now."

"Which way?" asked Denton again, mighty brief.

"Well," said I, "there's one thing I've always noticed in case of folks held up by the desert: they generally go wandering about here and there looking for water until they die not far from where they got lost. And usually they've covered a heap of actual distance."

"That's so," agreed Denton.

"Now, I've always figured that it would be a good

deal better to start right out for some particular place, even if it's ten thousand miles away. A man is just as likely to strike water going in a straight line as he is going in a circle; and then, besides, he's getting somewhere."

" Correct," said Denton.

" So," I finished, " I reckon we'd better follow the coast south and try to get to Mollyhay."

" How far is that? " asked Schwartz.

" I don't rightly know. But somewheres between three and five hundred miles, at a guess."

At that he fell to glowering and glooming with himself, brooding over what a hard time it was going to be. That is the way with a German. First off he's plumb scared at the prospect of suffering anything, and would rather die right off than take long chances. After he gets into the swing of it, he behaves as well as any man.

We took stock of what we had to depend on. The total assets proved to be just three pairs of legs. A pot of coffee had been on the fire, but that villain had kicked it over when he left. The kettle of beans was there, but somehow we got the notion they might have been poisoned, so we left them. I don't know

now why we were so foolish—if poison was his game, he'd have tried it before—but at that time it seemed reasonable enough. Perhaps the horror of the morning's work, and the sight of the brittle-brown mountains, and the ghastly yellow glare of the sun, and the blue waves racing by outside, and the big strong wind that blew through us so hard that it seemed to blow empty our souls, had turned our judgment. Anyway, we left a full meal there in the beanpot.

So without any further delay we set off up the ridge I had started to cross that morning. Schwartz lagged, sulky as a muley cow, but we managed to keep him with us. At the top of the ridge we took our bearings for the next deep bay. Already we had made up our minds to stick to the sea-coast, both on account of the lower country over which to travel and the off chance of falling in with a fishing vessel. Schwartz muttered something about its being too far even to the next bay, and wanted to sit down on a rock. Denton didn't say anything, but he jerked Schwartz up by the collar so fiercely that the German gave it over and came along.

We dropped down into the gully, stumbled over

the boulder wash, and began to toil in the ankle-deep sand of a little sage-brush flat this side of the next ascent. Schwartz followed steadily enough now, but had fallen forty or fifty feet behind. This was a nuisance, as we had to keep turning to see if he still kept up. Suddenly he seemed to disappear.

Denton and I hurried back to find him on his hands and knees behind a sage-brush, clawing away at the sand like mad.

"Can't be water on this flat," said Denton; " he must have gone crazy."

"What's the matter, Schwartz?" I asked.

For answer he moved a little to one side, showing beneath his knee one corner of a wooden box sticking above the sand.

At this we dropped beside him, and in five minutes had uncovered the whole of the chest. It was not very large, and was locked. A rock from the wash fixed that, however. We threw back the lid.

It was full to the brim of gold coins, thrown in loose, nigh two bushels of them.

"The treasure!" I cried.

There it was, sure enough, or some of it. We looked the chest through, but found nothing but the gold coins. The altar ornaments and jewels were lacking.

" Probably buried in another box or so," said Denton.

Schwartz wanted to dig around a little.

" No good," said I. " We've got our work cut out for us as it is."

Denton backed me up. We were both old hands at the business, had each in our time suffered the " cotton-mouth " thirst, and the memory of it outweighed any desire for treasure.

But Schwartz was money-mad. Left to himself he would have staid on that sand flat to perish, as certainly as had poor Billy. We had fairly to force him away, and then succeeded only because we let him fill all his pockets to bulging with the coins. As we moved up the next rise, he kept looking back and uttering little moans against the crime of leaving it.

Luckily for us it was winter. We shouldn't have lasted six hours at this time of year. As it was, the sun was hot against the shale and the little stones of those cussed hills. We plodded along until late afternoon, toiling up one hill and down another, only to repeat immediately. Towards sundown we made the second bay, where we plunged into the sea, clothes and all, and were greatly refreshed. I suppose a man absorbs a good deal that way. Anyhow, it always seemed to help.

We were now pretty hungry, and, as we walked along the shore, we began to look for turtles or shell-fish, or anything else that might come handy. There was nothing. Schwartz wanted to stop for a night's rest, but Denton and I knew better than that.

"Look here, Schwartz," said Denton, " you don't realise you're entered against time in this race—and that you're a damn fool to carrv all that weight in your clothes."

So we dragged along all night.

It was weird enough, I can tell you. The moon shone cold and white over that dead, drv country. Hot whiffs rose from the baked stones and hillsides. Shadows lay under the stones like animals crouching. When we came to the edge of a silvery hill we dropped off into pitchy blackness. There we stumbled over boulders for a minute or so, and began to climb the steep shale on the other side. This was fearful work. The top seemed always miles away. By morning we didn't seem to have made much of anywhere. The same old hollow-looking mountains with the sharp edges stuck up in about the same old places.

We had got over being very hungry, and, though we were pretty dry, we didn't really suffer yet from thirst. About this time Denton ran across some fish-hook cactus, which we cut up and chewed. They have a sticky wet sort of inside, which doesn't quench your thirst any, but helps to keep you from drying up and blowing away.

All that day we plugged along as per usual. It was main hard work, and we got to that state where things are disagreeable, but mechanical. Strange to say, Schwartz kept in the lead. It seemed to me at the time that he was using more energy than the occasion called for—just as man runs faster before he comes to the giving-out point. However, the hours went by, and he didn't seem to get any more tired than the rest of us.

We kept a sharp lookout for anything to eat, but there was nothing but lizards and horned toads. Later we'd have been glad of them, but by that time we'd got out of their district. Night came. Just at sundown we took another wallow in the surf, and chewed some more fishhook cactus. When the moon came up we went on.

I'm not going to tell you how dead beat we got. We were pretty tough and strong, for all of us had been used to hard living, but after the third day without anything to eat and no water to drink, it came to be pretty hard going. It got to the point where we had to have some *reason* for getting out besides just keeping alive. A man would sometimes rather die than keep alive, anyway, if it came only to that. But I know I made up my mind I was going to get out so I could smash up that Anderson, and I reckon Denton had the same idea. Schwartz didn't say anything, but he pumped on ahead of us, his back bent over, and his clothes sagging and bulging with the gold he carried.

We used to travel all night, because it was cool, and rest an hour or two at noon. That is all the rest we did get. I don't know how fast we went; I'd got beyond that. We must have crawled along mighty slow, though, after our first strength gave out. The way I used to do was to collect myself with an effort, look around for my bearings, pick out a landmark a little distance off, and forget everything but it.

Then I'd plod along, knowing nothing but the sand and shale and slope under my feet, until I'd reached that landmark. Then I'd clear my mind and pick out another.

But I couldn't shut out the figure of Schwartz that way. He used to walk along just ahead of my shoulder. His face was all twisted up, but I remember thinking at the time it looked more as if he was worried in his mind than like bodily suffering. The weight of the gold in his clothes bent his shoulders over.

As we went on the country gradually got to be more mountainous, and, as we were steadily growing weaker, it did seem things were piling up on us. The eighth day we ran out of the fishhook cactus, and, being on a high promontory, were out of touch with the sea. For the first time my tongue began to swell a little. The cactus had kept me from that before. Denton must have been in the same fix, for he looked at me and raised one eyebrow kind of humorous.

Schwartz was having a good deal of difficulty to navigate. I will say for him that he had done well, but now I could see that his strength was going on him in spite of himself. He knew it, all right, for when we rested that day he took all the gold coins and spread them in a row, and counted them, and put them back in his pocket, and then all of a sudden snatched out two handfuls and threw them as far as he could.

"Too heavy," he muttered, but that was all he could bring himself to throw away.

All that night we wandered high in the air. I guess we tried to keep a general direction, but I don't know. Anyway, along late, but before moonrise— she was now on the wane—I came to, and found myself looking over the edge of a twenty-foot drop. Right below me I made out a faint glimmer of white earth in the starlight. Somehow it reminded me of a little trail I used to know under a big rock back in Texas.

"Here's a trail," I thought, more than half loco; "I'll follow it!"

At least that's what half of me thought. The other half was sensible, and knew better, but it seemed to be kind of standing to one side, a little scornful, watching the performance. So I slid and slipped down to the strip of white earth, and, sure enough, it was a trail. At that the loco half of me gave the sensible part the laugh. I followed the path twenty feet and came to a dark hollow under the rock, and in it a round pool of water about a foot across. They say a man kills himself drinking too much, after starving for water. That may be, but it didn't kill me, and I sucked up all I could hold. Perhaps the fishhook cactus had helped. Well, sir, it was surprising how that drink brought me around. A minute before I'd been on the edge of going plumb loco, and here I was as clear-headed as a lawyer.

I hunted up Denton and Schwartz. They drank themselves full, too. Then we rested. It was mighty hard to leave that spring——

Oh, we had to do it. We'd have starved sure, there. The trail was a game trail, but that did us no good, for we had no weapons. How we did wish for the coffeepot, so we could take some away. We filled our hats, and carried them about three hours, before the water began to soak through. Then we had to drink it in order to save it.

The country fairly stood up on end. We had to climb separate little hills so as to avoid rolling rocks down on each other. It took it out of us. About this time we began to see mountain sheep. They would come right up to the edges of the small cliffs to look at us. We threw stones at them, hoping to hit one in the forehead, but of course without any results.

The good effects of the water lasted us about a day. Then we began to see things again. Off and on I could see water plain as could be in every hollow, and game of all kinds standing around and looking at me. I knew these were all fakes. By making an effort I could swing things around to where they belonged. I used to do that every once in a while, just to be sure we weren't doubling back, and to look out for real water. But most of the time it didn't seem to be worth while. I just let all these visions riot around and have a good time inside me or outside me, whichever it was. I knew I could get rid of them any minute. Most of the time, if I was in any doubt, it was easier to throw a stone to see if the animals were real or not. The real ones ran away.

We began to see bands of wild horses in the uplands. One day both Denton and I plainly saw one with saddle marks on him. If only one of us had seen him, it wouldn't have counted much, but we both made him out. This encouraged us wonderfully, though I don't see why it should have. We had topped the high country, too, and had started down the other side of the mountains that ran out on the promontory. Denton and I were still navigating without any thought of giving up, but Schwartz was getting in bad shape. I'd hate to pack twenty pounds over that country even with rest, food, and water. He was toting it on nothing. We told him so, and he came to see it, but he never could persuade himself to get rid of the gold all at once. Instead he threw away the pieces one by one. Each sacrifice seemed to nerve him up for another heat. I can shut my eyes and see it now—the wide, glaring, yellow country, the pasteboard mountains, we three dragging along, and the fierce sunshine flashing from the doubloons as one by one they went spinning through the air.

CHAPTER FOURTEEN

THE CHEWED SUGAR CANE

" I'D like to have trailed you fellows," sighed a voice from the corner.

" Would you!" said Colorado Rogers grimly.

It was five days to the next water. But they were worse than the eight days before. We were lucky, however, for at the spring we discovered in a deep wash near the coast, was the dried-up skull of a horse. It had been there a long time, but a few shreds of dried flesh still clung to it. It was the only thing that could be described as food that had passed our lips since breakfast thirteen days before. In that time we had crossed the mountain chain, and had come again to the sea. The Lord was good to us. He sent us the water, and the horse's skull, and the smooth hard beach, without breaks or the necessity of climbing hills. And we needed it, oh, I promise you, we needed it!

I doubt if any of us could have kept the direction except by such an obvious and continuous landmark as the sea to our left. It hardly seemed worth while to focus my mind, but I did it occasionally just by way of testing myself. Schwartz still threw away his gold coins, and once, in one of my rare intervals of looking about me, I saw Denton picking them up. This surprised me mildly, but I was too tired to be very curious. Only now, when I saw Schwartz's arm sweep out in what had become a mechanical movement, I always took pains to look, and always I saw Denton search for the coin. Sometimes he found it, and sometimes he did not.

The figures of my companions and the yellow-brown tide sand under my feet, and a consciousness of the blue and white sea to my left, are all I remember, except when we had to pull ourselves together for the purpose of cutting fishhook cactus. I kept going, and I knew I had a good reason for doing so, but it seemed too much of an effort to recall what that reason was.

Schwartz threw away a gold piece as another man would take a stimulant. Gradually, without really thinking about it, I came to see this, and then went on to sabe why Denton picked up the coins; and a great admiration for Denton's cleverness seeped through me like water through the sand. He was saving the coins to keep Schwartz going. When the last coin went, Schwartz would give out. It all sounds queer now, but it seemed all right then—and it *was* all right, too.

So we walked on the beach, losing entire track of time. And after a long interval I came to myself to see Schwartz lying on the sand, and Denton standing over him. Of course we'd all been falling down a lot, but always before we'd got up again.

" He's give out," croaked Denton.

His voice sounded as if it was miles away, which surprised me, but, when I answered, mine sounded miles away, too, which surprised me still more.

Denton pulled out a handful of gold coins.

" This will buy him some more walk," said he gravely, " but not much."

I nodded. It seemed all right, this new, strange purchasing power of gold—it *was* all right, by God, and as real as buying bricks——

" I'll go on," said Denton, " and send back help. You come after."

" To Mollyhay," said I.

This far I reckon we'd hung onto ourselves because it was serious. Now I began to laugh. So did
Denton. We laughed and laughed.

> " A damn long way
> To Mollyhay,"

said I. Then we laughed some more, until the tears
ran down our cheeks, and we had to hold our poor
weak sides. Pretty soon we fetched up with a gasp.

> " A damn long way
> To Mollyhay,"

whispered Denton, and then off we went into more
shrieks. And when we would sober down a little, one
or the other of us would say it again;

> " A damn long way
> To Mollyhay,"

and then we'd laugh some more. It must have been
a sweet sight!

At last I realised that we ought to pull ourselves
together, so I snubbed up short, and Denton did
the same, and we set to laying plans. But every

minute or so one of us would catch on some word, and then we'd trail off into rhymes and laughter and repetition.

"Keep him going as long as you can," said Denton.

"Yes."

"And be sure to stick to the beach."

That far it was all right and clear-headed. But the word "beach" let us out.

> "I'm a peach
> Upon the beach,"

sings I, and there we were both off again until one or the other managed to grope his way back to common sense again. And sometimes we crow-hopped solemnly around and around the prostrate Schwartz like a pair of Injins.

But somehow we got our plan laid at last, slipped the coins into Schwartz's pocket, and said good-bye.

> "Old socks, good-bye,
> You bet I'll try,"

yelled Denton, and laughing fit to kill, danced off up the beach, and out into a sort of grey mist that shut off everything beyond a certain distance from me now.

So I kicked Schwartz, he felt in his pocket, threw a gold piece away, and " bought a little more walk."

My entire vision was fifty feet or so across. Beyond that was grey mist. Inside my circle I could see the sand quite plainly and Denton's footprints. If I moved a little to the left, the wash of the waters would lap under the edge of that grey curtain. If I moved to the right, I came to cliffs. The nearer I drew to them, the farther up I could see, but I could never see to the top. It used to amuse me to move this area of consciousness about to see what I could find. Actual physical suffering was beginning to dull, and my head seemed to be getting clearer.

One day, without any apparent reason, I moved at right angles across the beach. Directly before me lay a piece of sugar cane, and one end of it had been chewed.

Do you know what that meant? Animals don't cut sugar cane and bring it to the beach and chew one end. A new strength ran through me, and actually the grey mist thinned and lifted for a moment, until

I could make out dimly the line of cliffs and the tumbling sea.

I was not a bit hungry, but I chewed on the sugar cane, and made Schwartz do the same. When we went on I kept close to the cliff, even though the walking was somewhat heavier.

I remember after that its getting dark and then light again, so the night must have passed, but whether we rested or walked I do not know. Probably we did not get very far, though certainly we staggered ahead after sun-up, for I remember my shadow.

About midday, I suppose, I made out a dim trail leading up a break in the cliffs. Plenty of such trails we had seen before. They were generally made by peccaries in search of cast-up fish—I hope they had better luck than we.

But in the middle of this, as though for a sign, lay another piece of chewed sugar cane.

CHAPTER FIFTEEN

THE CALABASH STEW

I HAD agreed with Denton to stick to the beach, but Schwartz could not last much longer, and I had not the slightest idea how far it might prove to be to Mollyhay. So I turned up the trail.

We climbed a mountain ten thousand feet high. I mean that; and I know, for I've climbed them that high, and I know just how it feels, and how many times you have to rest, and how long it takes, and how much it knocks out of you. Those are the things that count in measuring height, and so I tell you we climbed that far. Actually I suppose the hill was a couple of hundred feet, if not less. But on account of the grey mist I mentioned, I could not see the top, and the illusion was complete.

We reached the summit late in the afternoon, for the sun was square in our eyes. But instead of blinding me, it seemed to clear my sight, so that I saw below me a little mud hut with smoke rising behind it, and a small patch of cultivated ground.

I'll pass over how I felt about it: they haven't made the words——

Well, we stumbled down the trail and into the hut. At first I thought it was empty, but after a minute I saw a very old man crouched in a corner. As I looked at him he raised his bleared eyes to me, his head swinging slowly from side to side as though with a kind of palsy. He could not see me, that was evident, nor hear me, but some instinct not yet decayed turned him toward a new presence in the room. In my wild desire for water I found room to think that here was a man even worse off than myself.

A vessel of water was in the corner. I drank it. It was more than I could hold, but I drank even after I was filled, and the waste ran from the corners of my mouth. I had forgotten Schwartz. The excess made me a little sick, but I held down what I had swallowed, and I really believe it soaked into my system as it does into the desert earth after a drought.

In a moment or so I took the vessel and filled it and gave it to Schwartz. Then it seemed to me that my responsibility had ended. A sudden great dreamy lassitude came over me. I knew I needed food, but

I had no wish for it, and no ambition to search it out. The man in the corner mumbled at me with his toothless gums. I remember wondering if we were all to starve there peacefully together—Schwartz and his remaining gold coins, the man far gone in years, and myself. I did not greatly care.

After a while the light was blotted out. There followed a slight pause. Then I knew that someone had flown to my side, and was kneeling beside me and saying liquid, pitying things in Mexican. I swallowed something hot and strong. In a moment I came back from wherever I was drifting, to look up at a Mexican girl about twenty years old.

She was no great matter in looks, but she seemed like an angel to me then. And she had sense. No questions, no nothing. Just business. The only thing she asked of me was if I understood Spanish.

Then she told me that her brother would be back soon, that they were very poor, that she was sorry she had no meat to offer me, that they were *very* poor, that all they had was *calabash*—a sort of squash. All this time she was hustling things together. Next thing I knew I had a big bowl of calabash stew between my knees.

Now, strangely enough, I had no great interest

in that calabash stew. I tasted it, sat and thought a while, and tasted it again. By and by I had emptied the bowl. It was getting dark. I was very sleepy. A man came in, but I was too drowsy to pay any attention to him. I heard the sound of voices. Then I was picked up bodily and carried to an out-building and laid on a pile of skins. I felt the weight of a blanket thrown over me——

I awoke in the night. Mind you, I had practically had no rest at all for a matter of more than two weeks, yet I woke in a few hours. And, remember, even in eating the calabash stew I had felt no hunger in spite of my long fast. But now I found myself ravenous. You boys do not know what hunger is. It *hurts*. And all the rest of that night I lay awake chewing on the rawhide of a pack-saddle that hung near me.

Next morning the young Mexican and his sister came to us early, bringing more calabash stew. I fell on it like a wild animal, and just wallowed in it, so eager was I to eat. They stood and watched me— and I suppose Schwartz, too, though I had now lost interest in anyone but myself—glancing at each other in pity from time to time.

When I had finished the man told me that they

had decided to kill a beef so we could have meat. They were very poor, but God had brought us to them——

I appreciated this afterward. At the time I merely caught at the word "meat." It seemed to me I could have eaten the animal entire, hide, hoofs, and tallow. As a matter of fact, it was mighty lucky they didn't have any meat. If they had, we'd probably have killed ourselves with it. I suppose the calabash was about the best thing for us under the circumstances.

The Mexican went out to hunt up his horse. I called the girl back.

"How far is it to Mollyhay?" I asked her.

"A league," said she.

So we had been near our journey's end after all, and Denton was probably all right.

The Mexican went away horseback. The girl fed us calabash. We waited.

About one o'clock a group of horsemen rode over the hill. When they came near enough I recognised Denton at their head. That man was of tempered steel——

They had followed back along the beach, caught

our trail where we had turned off, and so discovered us. Denton had fortunately found kind and intelligent people.

We said good-bye to the Mexican girl. I made Schwartz give her one of his gold pieces.

But Denton could not wait for us to say " hullo " even, he was so anxious to get back to town, so we mounted the horses he had brought us, and rode off, very wobbly.

We lived three weeks in Mollyhay. It took us that long to get fed up. The lady I stayed with made a dish of kid meat and stuffed olives——

Why, an hour after filling myself up to the muzzle I'd be hungry again, and scouting round to houses looking for more to eat!

We talked things over a good deal, after we had gained a little strength. I wanted to take a little flyer at Guaymas to see if I could run across this Handy Solomon person, but Denton pointed out that Anderson would be expecting just that, and would take mighty good care to be scarce. His idea was that we'd do better to get hold of a boat and some water casks, and lug off the treasure we had stumbled over. Denton told us that the idea of going back and scooping all that dinero up with a shovel had kept him going, just as the idea of getting even with Anderson had kept me going. Schwartz said that after he'd carried that heavy gold over the first day, he made up his mind he'd get the spending of it or bust. That's why he hated so to throw it away.

There were lots of fishing boats in the harbour, and we hired one, and a man to run it for next to nothing a week. We laid a course north, and in six days anchored in our bay.

I tell you it looked queer. There were the charred sticks of the fire, and the coffeepot lying on its side. We took off our hats at poor Billy's grave a minute, and then climbed over the *cholla*-covered hill carrying our picks and shovels, and the canvas sacks to take the treasure away in.

There was no trouble in reaching the sandy flat. But when we got there we found it torn up from one end to the other. A few scattered timbers and three empty chests with the covers pried off alone remained. Handy Solomon had been there before us.

We went back to our boat sick at heart. Nobody said a word. We went aboard and made our Greaser boatman head for Yuma. It took us a week to get there. We were all of us glum, but Denton was the worst of the lot. Even after we'd got back to town and fallen into our old ways of life, he couldn't seem to get over it. He seemed plumb possessed of gloom, and moped around like a chicken with the pip. This surprised me, for I didn't think the loss of money would hit him so hard. It didn't hit any of us very hard in those days.

One evening I took him aside and fed him a drink, and expostulated with him.

"Oh, *hell*, Rogers," he burst out, "I don't care about the loot. But, suffering cats, think how that fellow sized us up for a lot of pattern-made fools; and how right he was about it. Why all he did was to sail out of sight around the next corner. He knew we'd start across country; and we did. All we had to do was to lay low, and save our legs. He was *bound* to come back. And we might have nailed him when he landed."

"That's about all there was to it," concluded Colorado Rogers, after a pause, "—except that I've been looking for him ever since, and when I heard you singing that song I naturally thought I'd landed."

" And you never saw him again? " asked Windy Bill.

" Well," chuckled Rogers, " I did about ten year later. It was in Tucson. I was in the back of a store, when the door in front opened and this man came in. He stopped at the little cigar-case by the door. In about one jump I was on his neck. I jerked him over backwards before he knew what had struck him, threw him on his face, got my hands in his back-hair, and began to jump his features against the floor. Then all at once I noted that this man had two arms; so of course he was the wrong fellow. " Oh, excuse me," said I, and ran out the back door."

CHAPTER SIXTEEN

THE HONK-HONK BREED

It was Sunday at the ranch. For a wonder the weather had been favourable; the windmills were all working, the bogs had dried up, the beef had lasted over, the remuda had not strayed—in short, there was nothing to do. Sang had given us a baked bread-pudding with raisins in it. We filled it in—a wash basin full of it—on top of a few incidental pounds of *chile con*, baked beans, soda biscuits, "air tights," and other delicacies. Then we adjourned with our pipes to the shady side of the blacksmith's shop where we could watch the ravens on top the adobe wall of the corral. Somebody told a story about ravens. This led to road-runners. This suggested rattlesnakes. They started Windy Bill.

"Speakin' of snakes," said Windy, "I mind when they catched the great-granddaddy of all the bull-snakes up at Lead in the Black Hills. I was only a kid then. This wasn't no such tur'ble long a snake, but he was more'n a foot thick. Looked just like

a sahuaro stalk. Man name of Terwilliger Smith
catched it. He named this yere bullsnake Clarence,
and got it so plumb gentle it followed him everywhere. One day old P. T. Barnum come along and
wanted to buy this Clarence snake—offered Terwilliger a thousand cold—but Smith wouldn't part
with the snake nohow. So finally they fixed up a
deal so Smith could go along with the show. They
shoved Clarence in a box in the baggage car, but
after a while Mr. Snake gets so lonesome he gnaws
out and starts to crawl back to find his master. Just as
he is half-way between the baggage car and the
smoker, the couplin' give way—right on that heavy
grade between Custer and Rocky Point. Well, sir,
Clarence wound his head 'round one brake wheel
and his tail around the other, and held that train
together to the bottom of the grade. But it stretched
him twenty-eight feet and they had to advertise him
as a boa-constrictor."

Windy Bill's history of the faithful bullsnake
aroused to reminiscence the grizzled stranger, who
thereupon held forth as follows:

Wall, I've see things and I've heerd things, some

of them ornery, and some you'd love to believe, they was that gorgeous and improbable. Nat'ral history was always my hobby and sportin' events my special pleasure—and this yarn of Windy's reminds me of the only chanst I ever had to ring in business and pleasure and hobby all in one grand merry-go-round of joy. It come about like this:

One day, a few year back, I was sittin' on the beach at Santa Barbara watchin' the sky stay up, and wonderin' what to do with my year's wages, when a little squinch-eye round-face with big bow spectacles came and plumped down beside me.

"Did you ever stop to think," says he, shovin' back his hat, "that if the horse-power delivered by them waves on this beach in one single hour could be concentrated behind washin' machines, it would be enough to wash all the shirts for a city of four hundred and fifty-one thousand one hundred and thirty-six people?"

"Can't say I ever did," says I, squintin' at him sideways.

"Fact," says he, "and did it ever occur to you that if all the food a man eats in the course of a natural life could be gathered together at one time, it would fill a wagon-train twelve miles long?"

"You make me hungry," says I.

"And ain't it interestin' to reflect," he goes on, "that if all the finger-nail parin's of the human race for one year was to be collected and subjected to hydraulic pressure it would equal in size the pyramid of Cheops?"

"Look yere," says I, sittin' up, "did *you* ever pause to excogitate that if all the hot air you is dispensin' was to be collected together it would fill a balloon big enough to waft you and me over that Bullyvard of Palms to yonder gin mill on the corner?"

He didn't say nothin' to that—just yanked me to my feet, faced me towards the gin mill above mentioned, and exerted considerable pressure on my arm in urgin' of me forward.

"You ain't so much of a dreamer, after all," thinks I. "In important matters you are plumb decisive."

We sat down at little tables, and my friend ordered a beer and a chicken sandwich.

"Chickens," says he, gazin' at the sandwich, " is

a dollar apiece in this country, and plumb scarce. Did you ever pause to ponder over the returns chickens would give on a small investment? Say you start with ten hens. Each hatches out thirteen aigs, of which allow a loss of say six for childish accidents. At the end of the year you has eighty chickens. At the end of two years that flock has increased to six hundred and twenty. At the end of the third year——"

He had the medicine tongue! Ten days later him and me was occupyin' of an old ranch fifty mile from anywhere. When they run stage-coaches this joint used to be a road-house. The outlook was on about a thousand little brown foothills. A road two miles four rods two foot eleven inches in sight run by in front of us. It come over one foothill and disappeared over another. I know just how long it was, for later in the game I measured it.

Out back was about a hundred little wire chicken corrals filled with chickens. We had two kinds. That was the doin's of Tuscarora. My pardner called himself Tuscarora Maxillary. I asked him once if that was his real name.

"It's the realest little old name you ever heerd

tell of," says he. " I know, for I made it myself—
liked the sound of her. Parents ain't got no rights
to name their children. Parents don't have to be
called them names."

Well, these chickens, as I said, was of two kinds.
The first was these low-set, heavy-weight proposi-
tions with feathers on their laigs, and not much
laigs at that, called Cochin Chinys. The other was
a tall ridiculous outfit made up entire of bulgin'
breast and gangle laigs. They stood about two foot
and a half tall, and when they went to peck the
ground their tail feathers stuck straight up to the
sky. Tusky called 'em Japanese Games.

" Which the chief advantage of them chickens
is," says he, " that in weight about ninety per cent.
of 'em is breast meat. Now my idee is, that if we
can cross 'em with these Cochin Chiny fowls we'll
have a low-hung, heavy-weight chicken runnin'
strong on breast meat. These Jap Games is too
small, but if we can bring 'em up in size and shorten
their laigs, we'll shore have a winner."

That looked good to me, so we started in on that
idee. The theery was bully, but she didn't work out.
The first broods we hatched growed up with big

husky Cochin Chiny bodies and little short necks, perched up on laigs three foot long. Them chickens couldn't reach ground nohow. We had to build a table for 'em to eat off, and when they went out rustlin' for themselves they had to confine themselves to sidehills or flyin' insects. Their breasts was all right, though—" And think of them drumsticks for the boardin'-house trade!" says Tusky.

So far things wasn't so bad. We had a good grubstake. Tusky and me used to feed them chickens twict a day, and then used to set around watchin' the playful critters chase grasshoppers up an' down the wire corrals, while Tusky figgered out what'd happen if somebody was dumfool enough to gather up somethin' and fix it in baskets or wagons or such. That was where we showed our ignorance of chickens.

One day in the spring I hitched up, rustled a dozen of the youngsters into coops, and druv over to the railroad to make our first sale. I couldn't fold them chickens up into them coops at first, but then I stuck the coops up on aidge and they worked all right, though I will admit they was a comical sight. At the railroad one of them towerist trains had just slowed down to a halt as I come up, and the towerists

was paradin' up and down allowin' they was particular enjoyin' of the warm Californy sunshine. One
old terrapin, with grey chin whiskers, projected
over, with his wife, and took a peek through the
slats of my coop. He straightened up like someone
had touched him off with a red-hot poker.

"Stranger," said he, in a scared kind of whisper,
"what's them?"

"Them's chickens," says I.

He took another long look.

"Marthy," says he to the old woman, "this will
be about all! We come out from Ioway to see the
Wonders of Californy, but I can't go nothin'
stronger than this. If these is chickens, I don't want
to see no Big Trees."

Well, I sold them chickens all right for a dollar
and two bits, which was better than I expected, and
got an order for more. About ten days later I got
a letter from the commission house.

"We are returnin' a sample of your Arts and
Crafts chickens with the lovin' marks of the teeth
still onto him," says they. "Don't send any more
till they stops pursuin' of the nimble grasshopper.
Dentist bill will foller."

With the letter came the remains of one of the chickens. Tusky and I, very indignant, cooked her for supper. She was tough, all right. We thought she might do better biled, so we put her in the pot over night. Nary bit. Well, then we got interested. Tusky kep' the fire goin' and I rustled greasewood. We cooked her three days and three nights. At the end of that time she was sort of pale and frazzled, but still givin' points to three-year-old jerky on cohesion and other uncompromisin' forces of Nature. We buried her then, and went out back to recuperate.

There we could gaze on the smilin' landscape, dotted by about four hundred long-laigged chickens swoopin' here and there after grasshoppers.

"We got to stop that," says I.

"We can't," murmured Tusky, inspired. "We can't. It's born in 'em; it's a primal instinct, like the love of a mother for her young, and it can't be eradicated! Them chickens is constructed by a divine providence for the express purpose of chasin' grasshoppers, jest as the beaver is made for buildin' dams, and the cow-puncher is made for whisky and faro-games. We can't keep 'em from it. If we was to shut 'em in a dark cellar, they'd flop after imag-

inary grasshoppers in their dreams, and die emaci-
ated in the midst of plenty. Jimmy, we're up agin
the Cosmos, the oversoul——" Oh, he had the medicine tongue, Tusky had, and risin' on the wings of
eloquence that way, he had me faded in ten minutes.
In fifteen I was wedded solid to the notion that the
bottom had dropped out of the chicken business. I
think now that if we'd shut them hens up, we might
have—still, I don't know; they was a good deal in
what Tusky said.

"Tuscarora Maxillary," says I, "did you ever
stop to entertain that beautiful thought that if all
the dumfoolishness possessed now by the human race
could be gathered together, and lined up alongside
of us, the first feller to come along would say to it
' Why, hello, Solomon!'"

We quit the notion of chickens for profit right
then and there, but we couldn't quit the place. We
hadn't much money, for one thing, and then we kind
of liked loafin' around and raisin' a little garden
truck, and—oh, well, I might as well say so, we had
a notion about placers in the dry wash back of the
house—you know how it is. So we stayed on, and
kept a-raisin' these long-laigs for the fun of it. I

used to like to watch 'em projectin' around, and I fed 'em twict a day about as usual.

So Tusky and I lived alone there together, happy as ducks in Arizona. About onc't in a month somebody'd pike along the road. She wasn't much of a road, generally more chuck-holes than bumps, though sometimes it was the other way around. Unless it happened to be a man horseback or maybe a freighter without the fear of God in his soul, we didn't have no words with them; they was too busy cussin' the highways and generally too mad for social discourses.

One day early in the year, when the 'dobe mud made ruts to add to the bumps, one of these automobeels went past. It was the first Tusky and me had seen in them parts, so we run out to view her. Owin' to the high spots on the road, she looked like one of these movin' picters, as to blur and wobble; sounded like a cyclone mingled with cuss-words, and smelt like hell on housecleanin' day.

"Which them folks don't seem to be enjoyin' of the scenery," says I to Tusky. "Do you reckon that there blue trail is smoke from the machine or remarks from the inhabitants thereof?"

Tusky raised his head and sniffed long and in-quirin'.

"It's langwidge," says he. "Did you ever stop to think that all the words in the dictionary hitched end to end would reach——"

But at that minute I catched sight of somethin' brass lyin' in the road. It proved to be a curled-up sort of horn with a rubber bulb on the end. I squoze the bulb and jumped twenty foot over the remark she made.

"Jarred off the machine," says Tusky.

"Oh, did it?" says I, my nerves still wrong. "I thought maybe it had growed up from the soil like a toadstool."

About this time we abolished the wire chicken corrals, because we needed some of the wire. Them long-laigs thereupon scattered all over the flat searchin' out their prey. When feed time come I had to screech my lungs out gettin' of 'em in, and then sometimes they didn't all hear. It was plumb dis-couragin', and I mighty nigh made up my mind to quit 'em, but they had come to be sort of pets, and I hated to turn 'em down. It used to tickle Tusky almost to death to see me out there hollerin' away like an old bull-frog. He used to come out reg'lar, with his pipe lit, just to enjoy me. Finally I got mad and opened up on him.

"Oh," he explains, "it just plumb amuses me to see the dumfool at his childish work. Why don't you teach 'em to come to that brass horn, and save your voice?"

"Tusky," says I, with feelin', "sometimes you do seem to get a glimmer of real sense."

Well, first off them chickens used to throw back-sommersets over that horn. You have no idee how slow chickens is to learn things. I could tell you things about chickens—say, this yere bluff about roosters bein' gallant is all wrong. I've watched 'em. When one finds a nice feed he gobbles it so fast that the pieces foller down his throat like yearlin's through a hole in the fence. It's only when he scratches up a measly one-grain quick-lunch that he calls up the hens and stands noble and self-sac-rificin' to one side. That ain't the point, which is, that after two months I had them long-laigs so they'd drop everythin' and come kitin' at the *honk-honk* of that horn. It was a purty sight to see 'em, sailin' in from all directions twenty foot at a stride. I was

proud of 'em, and named 'em the Honk-honk Breed.
We didn't have no others, for by now the coyotes
and bob-cats had nailed the straight-breds. There
wasn't no wild cat or coyote could catch one of my
Honk-honks, no, sir!

We made a little on our placer—just enough to
keep interested. Then the supervisors decided to fix
our road, and what's more, *they done it!* That's the
only part in this yarn that's hard to believe, but,
boys, you'll have to take it on faith. They ploughed
her, and crowned her, and scraped her, and rolled
her, and when they moved on we had the fanciest
highway in the State of Californy.

That noon—the day they called her a job—Tusky
and I sat smokin' our pipes as per usual, when
way over the foothills we seen a cloud of dust and
faint to our ears was bore a whizzin' sound. The
chickens was gathered under the cottonwood for the
heat of the day, but they didn't pay no attention.
Then faint, but clear, we heard another of them
brass horns:

"Honk! honk!" says it, and every one of them
chickens woke up, and stood at attention.

"Honk! honk!" it hollered clearer and nearer

Then over the hill come an automobeel, blowin' vigorous at every jump.

"My God!" I yells to Tusky, kickin' over my chair, as I springs to my feet. "Stop 'em! Stop 'em!"

But it was too late. Out the gate sprinted them poor devoted chickens, and up the road they trailed in vain pursuit. The last we seen of 'em was a minglin' of dust and dim figgers goin' thirty mile an hour after a disappearin' automobeel.

That was all we seen for the moment. About three o'clock the first straggler came limpin' in, his wings hangin', his mouth open, his eyes glazed with the heat. By sundown fourteen had returned. All the rest had disappeared utter; we never seen 'em again. I reckon they just naturally run themselves into a sunstroke and died on the road.

It takes a long time to learn a chicken a thing, but a heap longer to unlearn him. After that two or three of these yere automobeels went by every day, all a-blowin' of their horns, all kickin' up a hell of a dust. And every time them fourteen Honk-honks of mine took along after 'em, just as I'd taught 'em to do, layin' to get to their corn when they caught up. No more of 'em died, but that four-teen did get into elegant trainin'. After a while they got plumb to enjoyin' it. When you come right down to it, a chicken don't have many amusements and relaxations in this life. Searchin' for worms, chasin' grasshoppers, and wallerin' in the dust is about the limits of joys for chickens.

It was sure a fine sight to see 'em after they got well into the game. About nine o'clock every mornin' they would saunter down to the rise of the road where they would wait patient until a machine came along. Then it would warm your heart to see the enthusiasm of them. With exultant cackles of joy they'd trail in, reachin' out like quarter-horses, their wings half spread out, their eyes beamin' with delight. At the lower turn they'd quit. Then, after talkin' it over excited-like for a few minutes, they'd calm down and wait for another.

After a few months of this sort of trainin' they got purty good at it. I had one two-year-old rooster that made fifty-four mile an hour behind one of those sixty-horsepower Panhandles. When cars didn't come along often enough, they'd all turn out and chase jack-rabbits. They wasn't much fun at that. After a short, brief sprint the rabbit would crouch down plumb terrified, while the Honk-honks pulled off triumphal dances around his shrinkin' form.

Our ranch got to be purty well known them days among automobeelists. The strength of their cars was horse-power, of course, but the speed of them they got to ratin' by chicken-power. Some of them used to come way up from Los Angeles just to try out a new car along our road with the Honk-honks for pace-makers. We charged them a little somethin', and then, too, we opened up the road-house and the bar, so we did purty well. It wasn't necessary to work any longer at that bogus placer. Evenin's we sat around outside and swapped yarns, and I bragged on my chickens. The chickens would gather round close to listen. They liked to hear their praises sung, all right. You bet they *sabe!* The only reason a chicken, or any other critter, isn't intelligent is because he hasn't no chance to expand.

Why, we used to run races with 'em. Some of us would hold two or more chickens back of a chalk line, and the starter'd blow the horn from a hundred yards to a mile away, dependin' on whether it was a sprint or for distance. We had pools on the results, gave odds, made books, and kept records. After the thing got knowed we made money hand over fist.

The stranger broke off abruptly and began to roll a cigarette.

" What did you quit it for, then? " ventured Charley, out of the hushed silence.

" Pride," replied the stranger solemnly. " Haughtiness of spirit."

" How so? " urged Charley, after a pause.

" Them chickens," continued the stranger, after a moment, " stood around listenin' to me a-braggin' of what superior fowls they was until they got all puffed up. They wouldn't have nothin' whatever to do with the ordinary chickens we brought in for eatin' purposes, but stood around lookin' bored when there wasn't no sport doin'. They got to be just like that Four Hundred you read about in the papers. It was one continual round of grasshopper balls, race meets, and afternoon hen-parties. They got idle and haughty, just like folks. Then come race suicide. They got to feelin' so aristocratic the hens wouldn't have no eggs."

Nobody dared say a word.

"Windy Bill's snake——" began the narrator genially.

"Stranger," broke in Windy Bill, with great emphasis, "as to that snake, I want you to understand this: yereafter in my estimation that snake is nothin' but an ornery angle-worm!"

PART II

THE TWO-GUN MAN

CHAPTER ONE

THE CATTLE RUSTLERS

Buck Johnson was American born, but with a black beard and a dignity of manner that had earned him the title of Señor. He had drifted into southeastern Arizona in the days of Cochise and Victorio and Geronimo. He had persisted, and so in time had come to control the water—and hence the grazing— of nearly all the Soda Springs Valley. His troubles were many, and his difficulties great. There were the ordinary problems of lean and dry years. There were also the extraordinary problems of devastating Apaches; rivals for early and ill-defined range rights—and cattle rustlers.

Señor Buck Johnson was a man of capacity, courage, directness of method, and perseverance. Especially the latter. Therefore he had survived to see the Apaches subdued, the range rights adjusted, his cattle increased to thousands, grazing the area of a principality. Now, all the energy and fire of his frontiersman's nature he had turned to wiping out the third uncertainty of an uncertain business. He found it a task of some magnitude.

For Señor Buck Johnson lived just north of that terra incognita filled with the mystery of a double chance of death from man or the flaming desert known as the Mexican border. There, by natural gravitation, gathered all the desperate characters of three States and two republics. He who rode into it took good care that no one should ride behind him, lived warily, slept light, and breathed deep when once he had again sighted the familiar peaks of Cochise's Stronghold. No one professed knowledge of those who dwelt therein. They moved, mysterious as the desert illusions that compassed them about. As you rode, the ranges of mountains visibly changed form, the monstrous, snaky, sea-like growths of the cactus clutched at your stirrup, mock lakes sparkled and dissolved in the middle distance, the sun beat hot and merciless, the powdered dry alkali beat hotly and mercilessly back—and strange, grim men, swarthy, bearded, heavily armed, with red-rimmed unshifting eyes, rode silently out of the mists of illusion to look on you steadily, and then to ride silently back into the desert haze. They might be only the herders of the gaunt cattle, or again they might belong to the Lost Legion that peopled the country. All you could know was that of the men who entered in, but few returned.

Directly north of this unknown land you encountered parallel fences running across the country. They enclosed nothing, but offered a check to the cattle drifting toward the clutch of the renegades, and an obstacle to swift, dashing forays.

Of cattle-rustling there are various forms. The boldest consists quite simply of running off a bunch of stock, hustling it over the Mexican line, and there selling it to some of the big Sonora ranch owners. Generally this sort means war. Also are there subtler means, grading in skill from the rebranding through a wet blanket, through the crafty refashioning of a brand to the various methods of separating the cow from her unbranded calf. In the course of his task Señor Buck Johnson would have to do with them all, but at present he existed in a state of warfare, fighting an enemy who stole as the Indians used to steal.

Already he had fought two pitched battles, and

had won them both. His cattle increased, and he became rich. Nevertheless he knew that constantly his resources were being drained. Time and again he and his new Texas foreman, Jed Parker, had followed the trail of a stampeded bunch of twenty or thirty, followed them on down through the Soda Springs Valley to the cut drift fences, there to abandon them. For, as yet, an armed force would be needed to penetrate the borderland. Once he and his men had experienced the glory of a night pursuit. Then, at the drift fences, he had fought one of his battles. But it was impossible adequately to patrol all parts of a range bigger than some Eastern States.

Buck Johnson did his best, but it was like stopping with sand the innumerable little leaks of a dam. Did his riders watch toward the Chiricahuas, then a score of beef steers disappeared from Grant's Pass forty miles away. Pursuit here meant leaving cattle unguarded there. It was useless, and the Señor soon perceived that sooner or later he must strike in offence.

For this purpose he began slowly to strengthen the forces of his riders. Men were coming in from

Texas. They were good men, addicted to the grass-rope, the double cinch, and the ox-bow stirrup. Señor Johnson wanted men who could shoot, and he got them.

"Jed," said Señor Johnson to his foreman, "the next son of a gun that rustles any of our cows is sure loading himself full of trouble. We'll hit his trail and will stay with it, and we'll reach his cattle-rustling conscience with a rope."

So it came about that a little army crossed the drift fences and entered the border country. Two days later it came out, and mighty pleased to be able to do so. The rope had not been used.

The reason for the defeat was quite simple. The thief had run his cattle through the lava beds where the trail at once became difficult to follow. This delayed the pursuing party; they ran out of water, and, as there was among them not one man well enough acquainted with the country to know where to find more, they had to return.

"No use, Buck," said Jed. "We'd any of us come in on a gun play, but we can't buck the desert. We'll have to get someone who knows the country."

"That's all right—but where?" queried Johnson.

"There's Pereza," suggested Parker. "It's the only town down near that country."

"Might get someone there," agreed the Señor.

Next day he rode away in search of a guide. The third evening he was back again, much discouraged.

"The country's no good," he explained. "The regular inhabitants 're a set of Mexican bums and old soaks. The cowmen's all from north and don't know nothing more than we do. I found lots who claimed to know that country, but when I told 'em what I wanted they shied like a colt. I couldn't hire 'em, for no money, to go down in that country. They ain't got the nerve. I took two days to her, too, and rode out to a ranch where they said a man lived who knew all about it down there. Nary riffle. Man looked all right, but his tail went down like the rest when I told him what we wanted. Seemed plumb scairt to death. Says he lives too close to the gang. Says they'd wipe him out sure if he done it. Seemed plumb *scairt*." Buck Johnson grinned. "I told him so and he got hosstyle right off. Didn't seem no ways scairt of me. I don't know what's the matter with that outfit down there. They're plumb terrorised."

That night a bunch of steers was stolen from the very corrals of the home ranch. The home ranch was far north, near Fort Sherman itself, and so had always been considered immune from attack. Consequently these steers were very fine ones.

For the first time Buck Johnson lost his head and his dignity. He ordered the horses.

" I'm going to follow that —— —— into Sonora," he shouted to Jed Parker. " This thing's got to stop! "

" You can't make her, Buck," objected the fore-man. " You'll get held up by the desert, and, if that don't finish you, they'll tangle you up in all those little mountains down there, and ambush you, and massacre you. You know it damn well."

" I don't give a ——," exploded Señor John-son, " if they do. No man can slap my face and not get a run for it."

Jed Parker communed with himself.

" Señor," said he, at last, " it's no good; you can't do it. You got to have a guide. You wait three days and I'll get you one."

" You can't do it," insisted the Señor. " I tried every man in the district."

" Will you wait three days? " repeated the fore-man.

Johnson pulled loose his latigo. His first anger had cooled.

" All right," he agreed, " and you can say for me that I'll pay five thousand dollars in gold and give all the men and horses he needs to the man who has the nerve to get back that bunch of cattle, and bring in the man who rustled them. I'll sure make this a test case."

So Jed Parker set out to discover his man with nerve.

CHAPTER TWO

THE MAN WITH NERVE

At about ten o'clock of the Fourth of July a rider topped the summit of the last swell of land, and loped his animal down into the single street of Pereza. The buildings on either side were flat-roofed and coated with plaster. Over the sidewalks extended wooden awnings, beneath which opened very wide doors into the coolness of saloons. Each of these places ran a bar, and also games of roulette, faro, craps, and stud poker. Even this early in the morning every game was patronised.

The day was already hot with the dry, breathless, but exhilarating, heat of the desert. A throng of men idling at the edge of the sidewalks, jostling up and down their centre, or eddying into the places of amusement, acknowledged the power of summer by loosening their collars, carrying their coats on their arms. They were as yet busily engaged in recognising acquaintances. Later they would drink freely and gamble, and perhaps fight. Toward all but those whom they recognised they preserved an attitude of potential suspicion, for here were gathered the " bad men " of the border countries. A certain jealousy or touchy egotism lest the other man be considered quicker on the trigger, bolder, more aggressive than himself, kept each strung to tension. An occasional shot attracted little notice. Men in the cow-countries shoot as casually as we strike matches, and some subtle instinct told them that the reports were harmless.

As the rider entered the one street, however, a more definite cause of excitement drew the loose population toward the centre of the road. Immediately their mass blotted out what had interested them. Curiosity attracted the saunterers; then in turn the frequenters of the bars and gambling games. In a very few moments the barkeepers, gamblers, and look-out men, held aloof only by the necessities of their calling, alone of all the population of Pereza were not included in the newly-formed ring.

The stranger pushed his horse resolutely to the outer edge of the crowd where, from his point of vantage, he could easily overlook their heads. He was a quiet-appearing young fellow, rather neatly dressed in the border costume, rode a " centre fire," or single-cinch, saddle, and wore no chaps. He was what is known as a " two-gun man ": that is to say, he wore a heavy Colt's revolver on either hip. The fact that the lower ends of his holsters were tied down, in order to facilitate the easy withdrawal of the revolvers, seemed to indicate that he expected to use them. He had furthermore a quiet grey eye, with the glint of steel that bore out the inference of the tied holsters.

The newcomer dropped his reins on his pony's neck, eased himself to an attitude of attention, and looked down gravely on what was taking place.

He saw over the heads of the bystanders a tall, muscular, wild-eyed man, hatless, his hair rumpled into staring confusion, his right sleeve rolled to his shoulder, a wicked-looking nine-inch knife in his hand, and a red bandana handkerchief hanging by one corner from his teeth.

" What's biting the locoed stranger? " the young man inquired of his neighbour.

The other frowned at him darkly.

" Dare's anyone to take the other end of that

handkerchief in his teeth, and fight it out without letting go."

" Nice joyful proposition," commented the young man.

He settled himself to closer attention. The wild-eyed man was talking rapidly. What he said cannot be printed here. Mainly was it derogatory of the southern countries. Shortly it became boastful of the northern, and then of the man who uttered it. He swaggered up and down, becoming always the more insolent as his challenge remained untaken.

" Why don't you take him up? " inquired the young man, after a moment.

" Not me! " negatived the other vigorously. " I'll go yore little old gunfight to a finish, but I don't want any cold steel in mine. Ugh! it gives me the shivers. It's a reg'lar Mexican trick! With a gun it's down and out, but this knife work is too slow and searchin'."

The newcomer said nothing, but fixed his eye again on the raging man with the knife.

" Don't you reckon he's bluffing? " he inquired.

" Not any! " denied the other with emphasis. " He's jest drunk enough to be crazy mad."

The newcomer shrugged his shoulders and cast his glance searchingly over the fringe of the crowd. It rested on a Mexican.

"Hi, Tony! come here," he called.

The Mexican approached, flashing his white teeth.

"Here," said the stranger, "lend me your knife a minute."

The Mexican, anticipating sport of his own peculiar kind, obeyed with alacrity.

"You fellows make me tired," observed the stranger, dismounting. "He's got the whole townful of you bluffed to a standstill. Damn if I don't try his little game."

He hung his coat on his saddle, shouldered his way through the press, which parted for him readily, and picked up the other corner of the handkerchief.

"Now, you mangy son of a gun," said he.

CHAPTER THREE

THE AGREEMENT

JED PARKER straightened his back, rolled up the bandana handkerchief, and thrust it into his pocket, hit flat with his hand the tousselled mass of his hair, and thrust the long hunting knife into its sheath.

" You're the man I want," said he.

Instantly the two-gun man had jerked loose his weapons and was covering the foreman.

" *Am* I!" he snarled.

" Not jest that way," explained Parker. " My gun is on my hoss, and you can have this old toad-sticker if you want it. I been looking for you, and took this way of finding you. Now, let's go talk."

The stranger looked him in the eye for nearly a half minute without lowering his revolvers.

" I go you," said he briefly, at last.

But the crowd, missing the purport, and in fact the very occurrence of this colloquy, did not understand. It thought the bluff had been called, and

254

naturally, finding harmless what had intimidated it, gave way to an exasperated impulse to get even.

" You —— —— bluffer! " shouted a voice, " don't you think you can run any such ranikaboo here! "

Jed Parker turned humorously to his companion.

" Do we get that talk? " he inquired gently.

For answer the two-gun man turned and walked steadily in the direction of the man who had shouted. The latter's hand strayed uncertainly toward his own weapon, but the movement paused when the stranger's clear, steel eye rested on it.

" This gentleman," pointed out the two-gun man softly, " is an old friend of mine. Don't you get to calling of him names."

His eye swept the bystanders calmly.

" Come on, Jack," said he, addressing Parker.

On the outskirts he encountered the Mexican from whom he had borrowed the knife.

" Here, Tony," said he with a slight laugh, " here's a *peso*. You'll find your knife back there where I had to drop her."

He entered a saloon, nodded to the proprietor, and led the way through it to a box-like room containing a board table and two chairs.

" Make good," he commanded briefly.

" I'm looking for a man with nerve," explained Parker, with equal succinctness. " You're the man."

" Well? "

" Do you know the country south of here? "

The stranger's eyes narrowed.

" Proceed," said he.

" I'm foreman of the Lazy Y of Soda Springs Valley range," explained Parker. " I'm looking for a man with sand enough and *sabe* of the country enough to lead a posse after cattle-rustlers into the border country."

" I live in this country," admitted the stranger.

" So do plenty of others, but their eyes stick out like two raw oysters when you mention the border country. Will you tackle it? "

" What's the proposition? "

" Come and see the old man. He'll put it to you."

They mounted their horses and rode the rest of the day. The desert compassed them about, marvellously changing shape and colour, and every character, with all the noiselessness of phantasmagoria. At evening the desert stars shone steady and unwinking,

like the flames of candles. By moonrise they came
to the home ranch.

The buildings and corrals lay dark and silent
against the moonlight that made of the plain a sea
of mist. The two men unsaddled their horses and
turned them loose in the wire-fenced " pasture,"
the necessary noises of their movements sounding
sharp and clear against the velvet hush of the night.
After a moment they walked stiffly past the sheds
and cook shanty, past the men's bunk houses, and
the tall windmill silhouetted against the sky, to the
main building of the home ranch under its great
cottonwoods. There a light still burned, for this
was the third day, and Buck Johnson awaited his
foreman.

Jed Parker pushed in without ceremony.

" Here's your man, Buck," said he.

The stranger had stepped inside and carefully
closed the door behind him. The lamplight threw
into relief the bold, free lines of his face, the details
of his costume powdered thick with alkali, the shiny
butts of the two guns in their open holsters tied at
the bottom. Equally it defined the resolute countenance of Buck Johnson turned up in inquiry. The

two men examined each other—and liked each other at once.

" How are you," greeted the cattleman.

" Good-evening," responded the stranger.

" Sit down," invited Buck Johnson.

The stranger perched gingerly on the edge of a chair, with an appearance less of embarrassment than of habitual alertness.

" You'll take the job? " inquired the Señor.

" I haven't heard what it is," replied the stranger.

" Parker here——? "

" Said you'd explain."

" Very well," said Buck Johnson. He paused a moment, collecting his thoughts. " There's too much cattle-rustling here. I'm going to stop it. I've got good men here ready to take the job, but no one who knows the country south. Three days ago I had a bunch of cattle stolen right here from the home-ranch corrals, and by one man, at that. It wasn't much of a bunch—about twenty head—but I'm going to make a starter right here, and now. I'm going to get that bunch back, and the man who stole them, if I have to go to hell to do it. And I'm going to do the same with every case of rustling that comes

up from now on. I don't care if it's only one cow,
I'm going to get it back—every trip. Now, I want
to know if you'll lead a posse down into the south
country and bring out that last bunch, and the
man who rustled them? "

" I don't know——" hesitated the stranger.

" I offer you five thousand dollars in gold if you'll
bring back those cows and the man who stole 'em,"
repeated Buck Johnson. " And I'll give you all the
horses and men you think you need."

" I'll do it," replied the two-gun man promptly.

" Good! " cried Buck Johnson, " and you better
start to-morrow."

" I shall start to-night—right now."

" Better yet. How many men do you want, and
grub for how long? "

" I'll play her a lone hand."

" Alone! " exclaimed Johnson, his confidence visibly cooling. " Alone! Do you think you can make
her? "

" I'll be back with those cattle in not more than
ten days."

" And the man," supplemented the Señor.

" And the man. What's more, I want that money

here when I come in. I don't aim to stay in this country over night."

A grin overspread Buck Johnson's countenance. He understood.

"Climate not healthy for you?" he hazarded. "I guess you'd be safe enough all right with us. But suit yourself. The money will be here."

"That's agreed?" insisted the two-gun man.

"Sure."

"I want a fresh horse—I'll leave mine—he's a good one. I want a little grub."

"All right. Parker'll fit you out."

The stranger rose.

"I'll see you in about ten days."

"Good luck," Señor Buck Johnson wished him.

CHAPTER FOUR

THE ACCOMPLISHMENT

THE next morning Buck Johnson took a trip down into the " pasture " of five hundred wire-fenced acres.

" He means business," he confided to Jed Parker, on his return. " That cavallo of his is a heap sight better than the Shorty horse we let him take. Jed, you found your man with nerve, all right. How did you do it? "

The two settled down to wait, if not with confidence, at least with interest. Sometimes, remembering the desperate character of the outlaws, their fierce distrust of any intruder, the wildness of the country, Buck Johnson and his foreman inclined to the belief that the stranger had undertaken a task beyond the powers of any one man. Again, remembering the stranger's cool grey eye, the poise of his demeanour, the quickness of his movements, and the two guns with tied holsters to permit of easy withdrawal, they were almost persuaded that he might win.

" He's one of those long-chance fellows," surmised Jed. " He likes excitement. I see that by the way he takes up with my knife play. He'd rather leave his hide on the fence than stay in the corral."

" Well, he's all right," replied Señor Buck Johnson, " and if he ever gets back, which same I'm some doubtful of, his dinero 'll be here for him."

In pursuance of this he rode in to Willets, where shortly the overland train brought him from Tucson the five thousand dollars in double eagles.

In the meantime the regular life of the ranch went on. Each morning Sang, the Chinese cook, rang the great bell, summoning the men. They ate, and then caught up the saddle horses for the day, turning those not wanted from the corral into the pasture. Shortly they jingled away in different directions, two by two, on the slow Spanish trot of the cowpuncher. All day long thus they would ride, without food or water for man or beast, looking the range, identifying the stock, branding the young calves, examining generally into the state of affairs, gazing always with grave eyes on the magnificent, flaming, changing, beautiful, dreadful desert of the Arizona plains. At evening when the coloured atmosphere, catching the last glow, threw across the Chiricahuas its veil of mystery, they jingled in again, two by two, untired, unhasting, the glory of the desert in their deep-set, steady eyes.

And all the day long, while they were absent, the cattle, too, made their pilgrimage, straggling in singly, in pairs, in bunches, in long files, leisurely, ruminantly, without haste. There, at the long troughs filled by the windmill or the blindfolded pump mule, they drank, then filed away again into the mists of the desert. And Señor Buck Johnson, or his foreman, Parker, examined them for their condition, noting the increase, remarking the strays from another range. Later, perhaps, they, too, rode abroad. The same thing happened at nine other ranches from five to ten miles apart, where dwelt other fierce, silent men all under the authority of Buck Johnson.

And when night fell, and the topaz and violet and saffron and amethyst and mauve and lilac had faded suddenly from the Chiricahuas, like a veil that has been rent, and the ramparts had become slate-grey and then black—the soft-breathed night wandered here and there over the desert, and the land fell under an enchantment even stranger than the day's.

So the days went by, wonderful, fashioning the ways and the characters of men. Seven passed. Buck Johnson and his foreman began to look for the stranger. Eight, they began to speculate. Nine, they doubted. On the tenth they gave him up—and he came.

They knew him first by the soft lowing of cattle. Jed Parker, dazzled by the lamp, peered out from the door, and made him out dimly turning the animals into the corral. A moment later his pony's hoofs impacted softly on the baked earth, he dropped from the saddle and entered the room.

"I'm late," said he briefly, glancing at the clock, which indicated ten; "but I'm here."

His manner was quick and sharp, almost breathless, as though he had been running.

"Your cattle are in the corral: all of them. Have you the money?"

"I have the money here," replied Buck Johnson, laying his hand against a drawer, "and it's ready for you when you've earned it. I don't care so much

for the cattle. What I wanted is the man who stole them. Did you bring him?"

"Yes, I brought him," said the stranger. "Let's see that money."

Buck Johnson threw open the drawer, and drew from it the heavy canvas sack.

"It's here. Now bring in your prisoner."

The two-gun man seemed suddenly to loom large in the doorway. The muzzles of his revolvers covered the two before him. His speech came short and sharp.

"I told you I'd bring back the cows and the one who rustled them," he snapped. "I've never lied to a man yet. Your stock is in the corral. I'll trouble you for that five thousand. I'm the man who stole your cattle!"

PART III
THE RAWHIDE

CHAPTER ONE

THE PASSING OF THE COLT'S FORTY-FIVE

THE man of whom I am now to tell you came to Arizona in the early days of Chief Cochise. He settled in the Soda Springs Valley, and there persisted in spite of the devastating forays of that Apache. After a time he owned all the wells and springs in the valley, and so, naturally, controlled the grazing on that extensive free range. Once a day the cattle, in twos and threes, in bands, in strings, could be seen winding leisurely down the deep-trodden and converging trails to the water troughs at the home ranch, there leisurely to drink, and then leisurely to drift away into the saffron and violet and amethyst distances of the desert. At ten other outlying ranches this daily scene was repeated. All these cattle belonged to the man, great by reason of his priority in the country, the balance of his even character, and the grim determination of his spirit.

When he had first entered Soda Springs Valley his companions had called him Buck Johnson. Since then his form had squared, his eyes had steadied to the serenity of a great authority, his mouth, shadowed by the moustache and the beard, had closed straight in the line of power and taciturnity. There was about him more than a trace of the Spanish. So now he was known as Señor Johnson, although in reality he was straight American enough.

Señor Johnson lived at the home ranch with a Chinese cook, and Parker, his foreman. The home ranch was of adobe, built with loopholes like a fort. In the obsolescence of this necessity, other buildings had sprung up unfortified. An adobe bunk-house for the cow-punchers, an adobe blacksmith shop, a long, low stable, a shed, a windmill and pond-like reservoir, a whole system of corrals of different sizes, a walled-in vegetable garden—these gathered to themselves cottonwoods from the moisture of their being, and so added each a little to the green spot in the desert. In the smallest corral, between the stable and the shed, stood a buckboard and a heavy wagon, the only wheeled vehicles about the place. Under the shed were rows of saddles, riatas, spurs

mounted with silver, bits ornamented with the same
metal, curved short irons for the range branding,
long, heavy " stamps " for the corral branding. Behind the stable lay the " pasture," a thousand acres
of desert fenced in with wire. There the hardy cow-
ponies sought out the sparse, but nutritious, bunch
grass, sixty of them, beautiful as antelope, for they
were the pick of Señor Johnson's herds.

And all about lay the desert, shimmering, changing, many-tinted, wonderful, hemmed in by the
mountains that seemed tenuous and thin, like beautiful mists, and by the sky that seemed hard and
polished like a turquoise.

Each morning at six o'clock the ten cow-punchers
of the home ranch drove the horses to the corral,
neatly roped the dozen to be " kept up " for that
day, and rewarded the rest with a feed of grain.
Then they rode away at a little fox trot, two by
two. All day long they travelled thus, conducting
the business of the range, and at night, having com-
pleted the circle, they jingled again into the corral.
At the ten other ranches this programme had been
duplicated. The half-hundred men of Señor Johnson's
outfit had covered the area of a European princi-

pality. And all of it, every acre, every spear of grass, every cactus prickle, every creature on it, practically belonged to Señor Johnson, because Señor Johnson owned the water, and without water one cannot exist on the desert.

This result had not been gained without struggle. The fact could be read in the settled lines of Señor Johnson's face, and the great calm of his grey eye. Indian days drove him often to the shelter of the loopholed adobe ranch house, there to await the soldiers from the Fort, in plain sight thirty miles away on the slope that led to the foot of the Chiricahuas. He lost cattle and some men, but the profits were great, and in time Cochise, Geronimo, and the lesser lights had flickered out in the winds of destiny. The sheep terror merely threatened, for it was soon discovered that with the feed of Soda Springs Valley grew a burr that annoyed the flocks beyond reason, so the bleating scourge swept by forty miles away. Cattle rustling so near the Mexican line was an easy matter. For a time Señor Johnson commanded an armed band. He was lord of the high, the low, and the middle justice. He violated international ethics, and for the laws of nations he substituted his own. One by one he annihilated the thieves of cattle, sometimes in open fight, but oftener by surprise and deliberate massacre. The country was delivered. And then, with indefatigable energy, Señor Johnson became a skilled detective. Alone, or with Parker, his foreman, he rode the country through, gathering evidence. When the evidence was unassailable he brought offenders to book. The rebranding through a wet blanket he knew and could prove; the earmarking of an unbranded calf until it could be weaned he understood; the paring of hoofs to prevent travelling he could tell as far as he could see; the crafty alteration of similar brands—as when a Mexican changed Johnson's Lazy Y (————) to a Dumb-bell Bar (⊃—⊂)—he saw through at a glance. In short, the hundred and one petty tricks of the sneak-thief he ferreted out, in danger of his life. Then he sent to Phœnix for a Ranger—and that was the last of the Dumb-bell Bar brand, or the (⊂——⊃) Three Link Bar brand, or the (⊳≤⊰) Hour Glass Brand, or a half dozen others. The Soda Springs Valley acquired a reputation for good order.

Señor Johnson at this stage of his career found

himself dropping into a routine. In March began
the spring branding, then the corralling and breaking of the wild horses, the summer range-riding, the
great fall round-up, the shipping of cattle, and the
riding of the winter range. This happened over and
over again.

You and I would not have suffered from ennui.
The roping and throwing and branding, the wild
swing and dash of handling stock, the mad races to
head the mustangs, the fierce combats to subdue these
raging wild beasts to the saddle, the spectacle of
the round-up with its brutish multitudes and its
graceful riders, the dust and monotony and excitement and glory of the Trail, and especially the
hundreds of incidental and gratuitous adventures of
bears and antelope, of thirst and heat, of the joy
of taking care of one's self—all these would have
filled our days with the glittering, changing throng
of the unusual.

But to Señor Johnson it had become an old story.
After the days of construction the days of accom-
plishment seemed to him lean. His men did the work
and reaped the excitement. Señor Johnson never
thought now of riding the wild horses, of swinging

the rope coiled at his saddle horn, or of rounding ahead of the flying herds. His inspections were business inspections. The country was tame. The leather chaps with the silver *conchas* hung behind the door. The Colt's forty-five depended at the head of the bed. Señor Johnson rode in mufti. Of his cowboy days persisted still the high-heeled boots and spurs, the broad Stetson hat, and the fringed buckskin gauntlets.

The Colt's forty-five had been the last to go. Finally one evening Señor Johnson received an express package. He opened it before the undemonstrative Parker. It proved to contain a pocket " gun "—a nickel-plated, thirty-eight calibre Smith & Wesson " five-shooter." Señor Johnson examined it a little doubtfully. In comparison with the six-shooter it looked like a toy.

" How do you like her? " he inquired, handing the weapon to Parker.

Parker turned it over and over, as a child a rattle. Then he returned it to its owner.

" Señor," said he, " if ever you shoot me with that little old gun, *and* I find it out the same day, I'll just raise hell with you! "

"I don't reckon she'd *injure* a man much," agreed the Señor, "but perhaps she'd call his attention."

However, the "little old gun" took its place, not in Señor Johnson's hip pocket, but inside the front waistband of his trousers, and the old shiny Colt's forty-five, with its worn leather "Texas style" holster, became a bedroom ornament.

Thus, from a frontiersman dropped Señor Johnson to the status of a property owner. In a general way he had to attend to his interests before the cattlemen's association; he had to arrange for the buying and shipping, and the rest was leisure. He could now have gone away somewhere as far as time went. So can a fish live in trees—as far as time goes. And in the daily riding, riding, riding over the range he found the opportunity for abstract thought which the frontier life had crowded aside.

CHAPTER TWO

THE SHAPES OF ILLUSION

EVERY day, as always, Señor Johnson rode abroad over the land. His surroundings had before been accepted casually as a more or less pertinent setting of action and condition. Now he sensed some of the fascination of the Arizona desert.

He noticed many things before unnoticed. As he jingled loosely along on his cow-horse, he observed how the animal waded fetlock deep in the gorgeous orange California poppies, and then he looked up and about, and saw that the rich colour carpeted the landscape as far as his eye could reach, so that it seemed as though he could ride on and on through them to the distant Chiricahuas. Only, close under the hills, lay, unobtrusive, a narrow streak of grey. And in a few hours he had reached the streak of grey, and ridden out into it to find himself the centre of a limitless alkali plain, so that again it seemed the valley could contain nothing else of importance.

Looking back, Señor Johnson could discern a tenuous ribbon of orange—the poppies. And perhaps
ahead a little shadow blotted the face of the alkali,
which, being reached and entered, spread like fire
until it, too, filled the whole plain, until it, too, arro-
gated to itself the right of typifying Soda Springs
Valley as a shimmering prairie of mesquite. Flow-
ered upland, dead lowland, brush, cactus, volcanic
rock, sand, each of these for the time being occupied
the whole space, broad as the sea. In the circlet
of the mountains was room for many infinities.

Among the foothills Señor Johnson, for the first
time, appreciated colour. Hundreds of acres of flowers filled the velvet creases of the little hills and
washed over the smooth, rounded slopes so accurately
in the placing and manner of tinted shadows that
the mind had difficulty in believing the colour not to
have been shaded in actually by free sweeps of some
gigantic brush. A dozen shades of pinks and pur-
ples, a dozen of blues, and then the flame reds, the
yellows, and the vivid greens. Beyond were the
mountains in their glory of volcanic rocks, rich as
the tapestry of a Florentine palace. And, modify-
ing all the others, the tinted atmosphere of the south-

west, refracting the sun through the infinitesimal
earth motes thrown up constantly by the wind devils
of the desert, drew before the scene a delicate
and gauzy veil of lilac, of rose, of saffron, of amethyst, or of mauve, according to the time of day.
Señor Johnson discovered that looking at the landscape upside down accentuated the colour effects. It
amused him vastly suddenly to bend over his saddle horn, the top of his head nearly touching his
horse's mane. The distant mountains at once started
out into redder prominence; their shadows of purple
deepened to the royal colour; the rose veil thickened.

"She's the prettiest country God ever made!"
exclaimed Señor Johnson with entire conviction.

And no matter where he went, nor into how familiar country he rode, the shapes of illusion offered
always variety. One day the Chiricahuas were a
tableland; next day a series of castellated peaks;
now an anvil; now a saw tooth; and rarely they
threw a magnificent suspension bridge across the
heavens to their neighbours, the ranges on the west.
Lakes rippling in the wind and breaking on the
shore, cattle big as elephants or small as rabbits,
distances that did not exist and forests that never

were, beds of lava along the hills swearing to a cloud shadow, while the sky was polished like a precious stone—these, and many other beautiful and marvellous but empty shows the great desert displayed lavishly, with the glitter and inconsequence of a dream. Señor Johnson sat on his horse in the hot sun, his chin in his hand, his elbow on the pommel, watching it all with grave, unshifting eyes.

Occasionally, belated, he saw the stars, the wonderful desert stars, blazing clear and unflickering, like the flames of candles. Or the moon worked her necromancies, hemming him in by mountains ten thousand feet high through which there was no pass. And then as he rode, the mountains shifted like the scenes in a theatre, and he crossed the little sand dunes out from the dream country to the adobe corrals of the home ranch.

All these things, and many others, Señor Johnson now saw for the first time, although he had lived among them for twenty years. It struck him with the freshness of a surprise. Also it reacted chemically on his mental processes to generate a new power within him. The new power, being as yet unapplied, made him uneasy and restless and a little irritable.

He tried to show some of his wonders to Parker.

" Jed," said he, one day, " this is a great country."

" You *know* it," replied the foreman.

" Those tourists in their nickel-plated Pullmans call this a desert. Desert, hell! Look at them flowers!"

The foreman cast an eye on a glorious silken mantle of purple, a hundred yards broad.

" Sure," he agreed; " shows what we could do if we only had a little water."

And again: " Jed," began the Señor, "did you ever notice them mountains?"

" Sure," agreed Jed.

" Ain't that a pretty colour?"

" You bet," agreed the foreman; " now you're talking! I always said they was mineralised enough to make a good prospect."

This was unsatisfactory. Señor Johnson grew more restless. His critical eye began to take account of small details. At the ranch house one evening he, on a sudden, bellowed loudly for Sang, the Chinese servant.

" Look at these ! " he roared, when Sang appeared. Sang's eyes opened in bewilderment.

" There, and there ! " shouted the cattleman. " Look at them old newspapers and them gun rags ! The place is like a cow-yard. Why in the name of heaven don't you clean up here ! "

" Allee light," babbled Sang ; " I clean him."

The papers and gun rags had lain there unnoticed for nearly a year. Señor Johnson kicked them savagely.

" It's time we took a brace here," he growled " we're livin' like a lot of Oilers." [1]

[1] Oilers: Greasers—Mexicans

CHAPTER THREE

THE PAPER A YEAR OLD

SANG hurried out for a broom. Señor Johnson sat where he was, his heavy, square brows knit. Suddenly he stooped, seized one of the newspapers, drew near the lamp, and began to read.

It was a Kansas City paper and, by a strange coincidence, was dated exactly a year before. The sheet Señor Johnson happened to pick up was one usually passed over by the average newspaper reader. It contained only columns of little two- and three-line advertisements classified as Help Wanted, Situations Wanted, Lost and Found, and Personal. The latter items Señor Johnson commenced to read while awaiting Sang and the broom.

The notices were five in number. The first three were of the mysterious newspaper-correspondence type, in which Birdie beseeches Jack to meet her at the fountain; the fourth advertised a clairvoyant. Over the fifth Señor Johnson paused long. It reads

WANTED.—By an intelligent and refined lady of pleasing appearance, correspondence with a gentleman of means. Object matrimony.

Just then Sang returned with the broom and began noisily to sweep together the débris. The rustling of papers aroused Señor Johnson from his reverie. At once he exploded.

"Get out of here, you debased Mongolian," he shouted; "can't you see I'm reading?"

Sang fled, sorely puzzled, for the Señor was calm and unexcited and aloof in his everyday habit.

Soon Jed Parker, tall, wiry, hawk-nosed, deliberate, came into the room and flung his broad hat and spurs into the corner. Then he proceeded to light his pipe and threw the burned match on the floor.

"Been over to look at the Grant Pass range," he announced cheerfully. "She's no good. Drier than cork legs. Th' country wouldn't support three horned toads."

"Jed," quoth the Señor solemnly, "I wisht you'd hang up your hat like I have. It don't look good there on the floor."

"Why, sure," agreed Jed, with an astonished stare.

Sang brought in supper and slung it on the red and white squares of oilcloth. Then he moved the lamp and retired.

Señor Johnson gazed with distaste into his cup.

" This coffee would float a wedge," he commented sourly.

" She's no puling infant," agreed the cheerful Jed.

" And this!" went on the Señor, picking up what purported to be plum duff: " Bog down a few currants in dough and call her pudding!"

He ate in silence, then pushed back his chair and went to the window, gazing through its grimy panes at the mountains, ethereal in their evening saffron.

" Blamed Chink," he growled; " why don't he wash these windows? "

Jed laid down his busy knife and idle fork to gaze on his chief with amazement. Buck Johnson, the austere, the aloof, the grimly taciturn, the dangerous, to be thus complaining like a querulous woman!

" Señor," said he, " you're off your feed."

Señor Johnson strode savagely to the table and sat down with a bang.

" I'm sick of it," he growled; " this thing will

kill me off. I might as well go be a buck nun and be done with it."

With one round-arm sweep he cleared aside the dishes.

" Give me that pen and paper behind you," he requested.

For an hour he wrote and destroyed. The floor became littered with torn papers. Then he enveloped a meagre result. Parker had watched him in silence. The Señor looked up to catch his speculative eye. His own eye twinkled a little, but the twinkle was determined and sinister, with only an alloy of humour.

" Señor," ventured Parker slowly, " this event sure knocks me hell-west and crooked. If the loco you have culled hasn't paralysed your speaking parts, would you mind telling me what in the name of heaven, hell, and high-water is up? "

" I am going to get married," announced the Señor calmly.

" What! " shouted Parker; " who to? "

" To a lady," replied the Señor, " an intelligent and refined lady—of pleasing appearance."

CHAPTER FOUR

DREAMS

ALTHOUGH the paper was a year old, Señor Johnson in due time received an answer from Kansas.
A correspondence ensued. Señor Johnson enshrined
above the big fireplace the photograph of a woman.
Before this he used to stand for hours at a time
slowly constructing in his mind what he had hitherto
lacked—an ideal of woman and of home. This ideal
he used sometimes to express to himself and to the
ironical Jed.

"It must sure be nice to have a little woman
waitin' for you when you come in off'n the desert."

Or: "Now, a woman would have them windows
just blooming with flowers and white curtains and
such truck."

Or: "I bet that Sang would get a wiggle on him
with his little old cleaning duds if he had a woman
ahold of his jerk line."

Slowly he reconstructed his life, the life of the
ranch, in terms of this hypothesised feminine influ-

ence. Then matters came to an understanding. Señor Johnson had sent his own portrait. Estrella Sands wrote back that she adored big black beards, but she was afraid of him, he had such a fascinating bad eye: no woman could resist him. Señor Johnson at once took things for granted, sent on to Kansas a preposterous sum of " expense " money and a railroad ticket, and raided Goodrich's store at Willets, a hundred miles away, for all manner of gaudy carpets, silverware, fancy lamps, works of art, pianos, linen, and gimcracks for the adornment of the ranch house. Furthermore, he offered wages more than equal to a hundred miles of desert to a young Irish girl, named Susie O'Toole, to come out as housekeeper, decorator, boss of Sang and another Chinaman, and companion to Mrs. Johnson when she should arrive.

Furthermore, he laid off from the range work Brent Palmer, the most skilful man with horses, and set him to " gentling " a beautiful little sorrel. A sidesaddle had arrived from El Paso. It was " centre fire," which is to say it had but the single horsehair cinch, broad, tasselled, very genteel in its suggestion of pleasure use only. Brent could be seen at all times of day, cantering here and there on the sorrel, a blanket tied around his waist to simulate the long riding skirt. He carried also a sulky and evil gleam in his eye, warning against undue levity.

Jed Parker watched these various proceedings sardonically.

Once, the baby light of innocence blue in his eye, he inquired if he would be required to dress for dinner.

" If so," he went on, " I'll have my man brush up my low-necked clothes."

But Señor Johnson refused to be baited.

" Go on, Jed," said he; " you know you ain't got clothes enough to dust a fiddle."

The Señor was happy these days. He showed it by an unwonted joviality of spirit, by a slight but evident unbending of his Spanish dignity. No longer did the splendour of the desert fill him with a vague yearning and uneasiness. He looked upon it confidently, noting its various phases with care, rejoicing in each new development of colour and light, of form and illusion, storing them away in his memory so that their recurrence should find him prepared to recognise and explain them. For soon he would have someone by his side with whom to appreciate them. In that sharing he could see the reason for them, the reason for their strange bitter-sweet effects on the human soul.

One evening he leaned on the corral fence, looking toward the Dragoons. The sun had set behind them. Gigantic they loomed against the western light. From their summits, like an aureola, radiated the splendour of the dust-moted air, this evening a deep umber. A faint reflection of it fell across the desert, glorifying the reaches of its nothingness.

" I'll take her out on an evening like this," quoth Señor Johnson to himself, " and I'll make her keep her eyes on the ground till we get right up by Running Bear Knob, and then I'll let her look up all to once. And she'll surely enjoy this life. I bet she never saw a steer roped in her life. She can ride with me every day out over the range and I'll show her the busting and the branding and that band of antelope over by the Tall Windmill. I'll teach her to shoot, too. And we can make little pack trips off in the hills when she gets too hot— up there by Deerskin Meadows 'mongst the high peaks."

He mused, turning over in his mind a new picture

of his own life, aims, and pursuits as modified by the sympathetic and understanding companionship of a woman. He pictured himself as he must seem to her in his different pursuits. The picturesqueness pleased him. The simple, direct vanity of the man —the wholesome vanity of a straightforward nature —awakened to preen its feathers before the idea of the mate.

The shadows fell. Over the Chiricahuas flared the evening star. The plain, self-luminous with the weird lucence of the arid lands, showed ghostly. Jed Parker, coming out from the lamp-lit adobe, leaned his elbows on the rail in silent company with his chief. He, too, looked abroad. His mind's eye saw what his body's eye had always told him were the insistent notes—the alkali, the cactus, the sage, the mesquite, the lava, the choking dust, the blinding heat, the burning thirst. He sighed in the dim half recollection of past days.

"I wonder if she'll like the country?" he hazarded.

But Señor Johnson turned on him his steady eyes, filled with the great glory of the desert.

"Like the country!" he marvelled slowly. "Of course! Why shouldn't she?"

CHAPTER FIVE

THE ARRIVAL

THE Overland drew into Willets, coated from engine to observation with white dust. A porter, in strange contrast of neatness, flung open the vestibule, dropped his little carpeted step, and turned to assist someone. A few idle passengers gazed out on the uninteresting, flat frontier town.

Señor Johnson caught his breath in amazement. "God! Ain't she just like her picture!" he exclaimed. He seemed to find this astonishing.

For a moment he did not step forward to claim her, so she stood looking about her uncertainly, her leather suit-case at her feet.

She was indeed like the photograph. The same full-curved, compact little figure, the same round face, the same cupid's bow mouth, the same appealing, large eyes, the same haze of doll's hair. In a moment she caught sight of Señor Johnson and took two steps toward him, then stopped. The Señor at once came forward.

"You're Mr. Johnson, ain't you?" she inquired, thrusting her little pointed chin forward, and so elevating her baby-blue eyes to his.

"Yes, ma'am," he acknowledged formally. Then, after a moment's pause: "I hope you're well."

"Yes, thank you."

The station loungers, augmented by all the ranchmen and cowboys in town, were examining her closely. She looked at them in a swift side glance that seemed to gather all their eyes to hers. Then, satisfied that she possessed the universal admiration, she returned the full force of her attention to the man before her.

"Now you give me your trunk checks," he was saying, "and then we'll go right over and get married."

"Oh!" she gasped.

"That's right, ain't it?" he demanded.

"Yes, I suppose so," she agreed faintly.

A little subdued, she followed him to the clergyman's house, where, in the presence of Goodrich, the storekeeper, and the preacher's wife, the two were united. Then they mounted the buckboard and drove from town.

Señor Johnson said nothing, because he knew of nothing to say. He drove skilfully and fast through the gathering dusk. It was a hundred miles to the home ranch, and that hundred miles, by means of five relays of horses already arranged for, they would cover by morning. Thus they would avoid the dust and heat and high winds of the day.

The sweet night fell. The little desert winds laid soft fingers on their cheeks. Overhead burned the stars, clear, unflickering, like candles. Dimly could be seen the horses, their flanks swinging steadily in the square trot. Ghostly bushes passed them; ghostly rock elevations. Far, in indeterminate distance, lay the outlines of the mountains. Always, they seemed to recede. The plain, all but invisible, the wagon trail quite so, the depths of space—these flung heavy on the soul their weight of mysticism. The woman, until now bolt upright in the buckboard seat, shrank nearer to the man. He felt against his sleeve the delicate contact of her garment and thrilled to the touch. A coyote barked sharply from a neighbouring eminence, then trailed off into the long-drawn, shrill howl of his species.

"What was that?" she asked quickly, in a sub-dued voice.

"A coyote—one of them little wolves," he ex-plained.

The horses' hoofs rang clear on a hardened bit of the alkali crust, then dully as they encountered again the dust of the plain. Vast, vague, mysterious in the silence of night, filled with strange influences breath-ing through space like damp winds, the desert took them to the heart of her great spaces.

"Buck," she whispered, a little tremblingly. It was the first time she had spoken his name.

"What is it?" he asked, a new note in his voice.

But for a time she did not reply. Only the con-tact against his sleeve increased by ever so little.

"Buck," she repeated, then all in a rush and with a sob, "Oh, I'm afraid."

Tenderly the man drew her to him. Her head fell against his shoulder and she hid her eyes.

"There, little girl," he reassured her, his big voice rich and musical. "There's nothing to get scairt of. I'll take care of you. What frightens you, honey?"

She nestled close in his arm with a sigh of half relief.

" I don't know," she laughed, but still with a tremble in her tones. " It's all so big and lonesome and strange—and I'm so little."

" There, little girl," he repeated.

They drove on and on. At the end of two hours they stopped. Men with lanterns dazzled their eyes. The horses were changed, and so out again into the night where the desert seemed to breathe in deep, mysterious exhalations like a sleeping beast.

Señor Johnson drove his horses masterfully with his one free hand. The road did not exist, except to his trained eyes. They seemed to be swimming out, out, into a vapour of night with the wind of their going steady against their faces.

" Buck," she murmured, " I'm so tired."

He tightened his arm around her and she went to sleep, half-waking at the ranches where the relays waited, dozing again as soon as the lanterns dropped behind. And Señor Johnson, alone with his horses and the solemn stars, drove on, ever on, into the desert.

By grey of the early summer dawn they arrived.

The girl wakened, descended, smiling uncertainly at Susie O'Toole, blinking somnolently at her surroundings. Susie put her to bed in the little southwest room where hung the shiny Colt's forty-five in its worn leather " Texas-style " holster. She murmured incoherent thanks and sank again to sleep, overcome by the fatigue of unaccustomed travelling, by the potency of the desert air, by the excitement of anticipation to which her nerves had long been strung.

Señor Johnson did not sleep. He was tough, and used to it. He lit a cigar and rambled about, now reading the newspapers he had brought with him, now prowling softly about the building, now visiting the corrals and outbuildings, once even the thousand-acre pasture where his saddle-horse knew him and came to him to have its forehead rubbed.

The dawn broke in good earnest, throwing aside its gauzy draperies of mauve. Sang, the Chinese cook, built his fire. Señor Johnson forbade him to clang the rising bell, and himself roused the cowpunchers. The girl slept on. Señor Johnson tiptoed a dozen times to the bedroom door. Once he ventured to push it open. He looked long within, then shut it softly and tiptoed out into the open, his eyes shining.

" Jed," he said to his foreman, " you don't know how it made me feel. To see her lying there so pink and soft and pretty, with her yaller hair all tumbled about and a little smile on her—there in my old bed, with my old gun hanging over her that way—— By Heaven, Jed, it made me feel almost *holy!* "

CHAPTER SIX

THE WAGON TIRE

About noon she emerged from the room, fully refreshed and wide awake. She and Susie O'Toole had unpacked at least one of the trunks, and now she stood arrayed in shirt-waist and blue skirt.

At once she stepped into the open air and looked about her with considerable curiosity.

"So this is a real cattle ranch," was her comment.

Señor Johnson was at her side pressing on her with boyish eagerness the sights of the place. She patted the stag hounds and inspected the garden. Then, confessing herself hungry, she obeyed with alacrity Sang's call to an early meal. At the table she ate coquettishly, throwing her birdlike side glances at the man opposite.

"I want to see a real cowboy," she announced, as she pushed her chair back.

"Why, sure!" cried Señor Johnson joyously. "Sang! hi, Sang! Tell Brent Palmer to step in here a minute."

After an interval the cowboy appeared, mincing in on his high-heeled boots, his silver spurs jingling, the fringe of his chaps impacting softly on the leather. He stood at ease, his broad hat in both hands, his dark, level brows fixed on his chief.

"Shake hands with Mrs. Johnson, Brent. I called you in because she said she wanted to see a real cow-puncher."

"Oh, *Buck!*" cried the woman.

For an instant the cow-puncher's level brows drew together. Then he caught the woman's glance fair. He smiled.

"Well, I ain't much to look at," he proffered.

"That's not for you to say, sir," said Estrella, recovering.

"Brent, here, gentled your pony for you," exclaimed Señor Johnson.

"Oh," cried Estrella, "have I a pony? How nice. And it was so good of you, Mr. Brent. Can't I see him? I want to see him. I want to give him a piece of sugar." She fumbled in the bowl.

"Sure you can see him. I don't know as he'll eat sugar. He ain't that educated. Think you could teach him to eat sugar, Brent?"

"I reckon," replied the cowboy.

They went out toward the corral, the cowboy joining them as a matter of course. Estrella demanded explanations as she went along. Their progress was leisurely. The blindfolded pump mule interested her.

" And he goes round and round that way all day without stopping, thinking he's really getting somewhere!" she marvelled. "I think that's a shame! Poor old fellow, to get fooled that way!"

" It is some foolish," said Brent Palmer, " but he ain't any worse off than a cow-pony that hikes out twenty mile and then twenty back

" No, I suppose not," admitted Estrella.

" And we got to have water, you know," added Señor Johnson.

Brent rode up the sorrel bareback. The pretty animal, gentle as a kitten, nevertheless planted his forefeet strongly and snorted at Estrella.

" I reckon he ain't used to the sight of a woman," proffered the Señor, disappointed. " He'll get used to you. Go up to him soft-like and rub him between the eyes."

Estrella approached, but the pony jerked back his head with every symptom of distrust. She forgot the sugar she had intended to offer him.

" He's a perfect beauty," she said at last, " but,

my! I'd never dare ride him. I'm awful scairt of horses."

"Oh, he'll come around all right," assured Brent easily. "I'll fix him."

"Oh, Mr. Brent," she exclaimed, "don't think I don't appreciate what you've done. I'm sure he's really just as gentle as he can be. It's only that I'm foolish."

"I'll fix him," repeated Brent.

The two men conducted her here and there, showing her the various institutions of the place. A man bent near the shed nailing a shoe to a horse's hoof.

"So you even have a blacksmith!" said Estrella. Her guides laughed amusedly.

"Tommy, come here!" called the Señor.

The horseshoer straightened up and approached. He was a lithe, curly-haired young boy, with a reckless, humorous eye and a smooth face, now red from bending over.

"Tommy, shake hands with Mrs. Johnson," said the Señor. "Mrs. Johnson wants to know if you're the blacksmith." He exploded in laughter.

"Oh, *Buck!*" cried Estrella again.

"No, ma'am," answered the boy directly; "I'm

just tacking a shoe on Danger, here. We all does our own blacksmithing."

His roving eye examined her countenance respectfully, but with admiration. She caught the admiration and returned it, covertly but unmistakably, pleased that her charms were appreciated.

They continued their rounds. The sun was very hot and the dust deep. A woman would have known that these things distressed Estrella. She picked her way through the débris; she dropped her head from the burning; she felt her delicate garments moistening with perspiration, her hair dampening; the dust sifted up through the air. Over in the large corral a broncho buster, assisted by two of the cowboys, was engaged in roping and throwing some wild mustangs. The sight was wonderful, but here the dust billowed in clouds.

"I'm getting a little hot and tired," she confessed at last. "I think I'll go to the house."

But near the shed she stopped again, interested in spite of herself by a bit of repairing Tommy had under way. The tire of a wagon wheel had been destroyed. Tommy was mending it. On the ground lay a fresh cowhide. From this Tommy was cutting a

wide strip. As she watched he measured the strip
around the circumference of the wheel.

" He isn't going to make a tire of that! " she exclaimed, incredulously.

" Sure," replied Señor Johnson.

" Will it wear? "

" It'll wear for a month or so, till we can get another from town."

Estrella advanced and felt curiously of the rawhide. Tommy was fastening it to the wheel at the
ends only.

" But how can it stay on that way? " she objected.
" It'll come right off as soon as you use it."

" It'll harden on tight enough."

" Why? " she persisted. " Does it shrink much
when it dries? "

Señor Johnson stared to see if she might be joking. " Does it shrink? " he repeated slowly. " There
ain't nothing shrinks more, nor harder. It'll mighty
nigh break that wood."

Estrella, incredulous, interested, she could not
have told why, stooped again to feel the soft, yield-
ing hide. She shook her head.

" You're joking me because I'm a tenderfoot,"
she accused brightly. " I know it dries hard, and I'll

believe it shrinks a lot, but to break wood—that's piling it on a little thick."

" No, that's right, ma'am," broke in Brent Palmer. "It's awful strong. It pulls like a horse when the desert sun gets on it. You wrap anything up in a piece of that hide and see what happens. Some time you take and wrap a piece around a potato and put her out in the sun and see how it'll squeeze the water out of her."

" Is that so? " she appealed to Tommy. " I can't tell when they are making fun of me."

" Yes, ma'am, that's right," he assured her.

Estrella passed a strip of the flexible hide playfully about her wrists.

" And if I let that dry that way I'd be handcuffed hard and fast," she said.

" It would cut you down to the bone," supplemented Brent Palmer.

She untwisted the strip, and stood looking at it, her eyes wide.

" I—I don't know why——" she faltered. " The thought makes me a little sick. Why, isn't it queer? Ugh! it's like a snake!" She flung it from her energetically and turned toward the ranch house.

CHAPTER SEVEN

ESTRELLA

THE honeymoon developed and the necessary adjustments took place. The latter Señor Johnson had not foreseen; and yet, when the necessity for them arose, he acknowledged them right and proper.

"Course she don't want to ride over to Circle I with us," he informed his confidant, Jed Parker. "It's a long ride, and she ain't used to riding yet. Trouble is I've been thinking of doing things with her just as if she was a man. Women are different. They likes different things."

This second idea gradually overlaid the first in Señor Johnson's mind. Estrella showed little aptitude or interest in the rougher side of life. Her husband's statement as to her being still unused to riding was distinctly a euphemism. Estrella never arrived at the point of feeling safe on a horse. In time she gave up trying, and the sorrel drifted back to cow-punching. The range work she never understood.

306

As a spectacle it imposed itself on her interest for a week; but since she could discover no real and vital concern in the welfare of cows, soon the mere outward show became an old story. Estrella's sleek nature avoided instinctively all that interfered with bodily well-being. When she was cool and well-fed and not thirsty, and surrounded by a proper degree of feminine daintiness, then she was ready to amuse herself. But she could not understand the desirability of those pleasures for which a certain price in discomfort must be paid. As for firearms, she confessed herself frankly afraid of them. That was the point at which her intimacy with them stopped.

The natural level to which these waters fell is easily seen. Quite simply, the Señor found that a wife does not enter fully into her husband's workaday life. The dreams he had dreamed did not come true.

This was at first a disappointment to him, of course, but the disappointment did not last. Señor Johnson was a man of sense, and he easily modified his first scheme of married life.

"She'd get sick of it, and I'd get sick of it," he formulated his new philosophy. "Now I got some-

thing to come back to, somebody to look forward **to.**
And it's a *woman;* it ain't one of these darn gangle-
leg cowgirls. The great thing is to feel you *belong*
to someone; and that someone nice and cool and
fresh and purty is waitin' for you when you come
in tired. It beats that other little old idee of mine
slick as a gun barrel."

So, during this, the busy season of the range riding, immediately before the great fall round-ups,
Señor Johnson rode abroad all day, and returned to
his own hearth as many evenings of the week as he
could. Estrella always saw him coming and stood in
the doorway to greet him. He kicked off his spurs,
washed and dusted himself, and spent the evening
with his wife. He liked the sound of exactly that
phrase, and was fond of repeating it to himself in
a variety of connections.

"When I get in I'll spend the evening with my
wife." "If I don't ride over to Circle I, I'll spend the
evening with my wife," and so on. He had a good
deal to tell her of the day's discoveries, the state of
the range, and the condition of the cattle. To all of
this she listened at least with patience. Señor Johnson, like most men who have long delayed marriage,

was self-centred without knowing it. His interest in his mate had to do with her personality rather than with her doings.

" What you do with yourself all day to-day? " he occasionally inquired.

" Oh, there's lots to do," she would answer, a trifle listlessly ; and this reply always seemed quite to satisfy his interest in the subject.

Señor Johnson, with a curiously instant transformation often to be observed among the adventurous, settled luxuriously into the state of being a married man. Its smallest details gave him distinct and separate sensations of pleasure.

" I plumb likes it all," he said. " I likes havin' interest in some fool geranium plant, and I likes worryin' about the screen doors and all the rest of the plumb foolishness. It does me good. It feels like stretchin' your legs in front of a good warm fire."

The centre, the compelling influence of this new state of affairs, was undoubtedly Estrella, and yet it is equally to be doubted whether she stood for more than the suggestion. Señor Johnson conducted his entire life with reference to his wife. His waking hours were concerned only with the thought of her, his every act revolved in its orbit controlled by her influence. Nevertheless she, as an individual human being, had little to do with it. Señor Johnson referred his life to a state of affairs he had himself invented and which he called the married state, and to a woman whose attitude he had himself determined upon and whom he designated as his wife. The actual state of affairs—whatever it might be—he did not see; and the actual woman supplied merely the material medium necessary to the reality of his idea. Whether Estrella's eyes were interested or bored, bright or dull, alert or abstracted, contented or afraid, Señor Johnson could not have told you. He might have replied promptly enough—that they were happy and loving. That is the way Señor Johnson conceived a wife's eyes.

The routine of life, then, soon settled. After breakfast the Señor insisted that his wife accompany him on a short tour of inspection. "A little *pasear*," he called it, "just to get set for the day." Then his horse was brought, and he rode away on whatever business called him. Like a true son of the alkali, he took no lunch with him, nor expected his horse to feed until his return. This was an hour before sunset. The evening passed as has been described. It was all very simple.

When the business hung close to the ranch house —as in the bronco busting, the rebranding of bought cattle, and the like—he was able to share his wife's day. Estrella conducted herself dreamily, with a slow smile for him when his actual presence insisted on her attention. She seemed much given to staring out over the desert. Señor Johnson, appreciatively, thought he could understand this. Again, she gave much leisure to rocking back and forth on the low, wide veranda, her hands idle, her eyes vacant, her lips dumb. Susie O'Toole had early proved incompatible and had gone.

" A nice, contented, home sort of a woman," said Señor Johnson.

One thing alone besides the desert, on which she never seemed tired of looking, fascinated her. Whenever a beef was killed for the uses of the ranch, she commanded strips of the green skin. Then, like a child, she bound them and sewed them and nailed them to substances particularly susceptible to their constricting power. She choked the necks of green gourds, she indented the tender bark of cottonwood shoots, she expended an apparently exhaustless ingenuity on the fabrication of mechanical devices whose principle answered to the pulling of the drying rawhide. And always along the adobe fence could be seen a long row of potatoes bound in skin, some of them fresh and smooth and round; some sweating in the agony of squeezing; some wrinkled and dry and little, the last drops of life tortured out of them. Señor Johnson laughed good-humouredly at these toys, puzzled to explain their fascination for his wife.

"They're sure an amusing enough contraption, honey," said he, "but what makes you stand out there in the hot sun staring at them that way? It's cooler on the porch."

"I don't know," said Estrella, helplessly, turning her slow, vacant gaze on him. Suddenly she shivered in a strong physical revulsion. "I don't know!" she cried with passion.

After they had been married about a month Señor Johnson found it necessary to drive into Willets.

"How would you like to go, too, and buy some duds?" he asked Estrella.

"Oh!" she cried strangely. "When?"

"Day after to-morrow."

The trip decided, her entire attitude changed. The vacancy of her gaze lifted; her movements quickened; she left off staring at the desert, and her rawhide toys were neglected. Before starting, Señor Johnson gave her a check book. He explained that there were no banks in Willets, but that Goodrich, the storekeeper, would honour her signature.

"Buy what you want to, honey," said he. "Tear her wide open. I'm good for it."

"How much can I draw?" she asked, smiling.

"As much as you want to," he replied with emphasis.

"Take care"—she poised before him with the check book extended—"I may draw—I might draw fifty thousand dollars."

"Not out of Goodrich," he grinned; "you'd bust the game. But hold him up for the limit, anyway."

He chuckled aloud, pleased at the rare, bird-like coquetry of the woman. They drove to Willets. It took them two days to go and two days to return. Estrella went through the town in a cyclone burst of enthusiasm, saw everything, bought everything, exhausted everything in two hours. Willets was not a large place. On her return to the ranch she sat down at once in the rocking-chair on the veranda. Her hands fell into her lap. She stared out over the desert.

Señor Johnson stole up behind her, clumsy as a playful bear. His eyes followed the direction of hers to where a cloud shadow lay across the slope, heavy, palpable, untransparent, like a blotch of ink.

" Pretty, isn't it, honey? " said he. " Glad to get back? "

She smiled at him her vacant, slow smile.

" Here's my check book," she said; " put it away for me. I'm through with it."

" I'll put it in my desk," said he. " It's in the left-hand cubby-hole," he called from inside.

" Very well," she replied.

He stood in the doorway, looking fondly at her unconscious shoulders and the pose of her blonde head thrown back against the high rocking-chair.

" That's the sort of a woman, after all," said Señor Johnson. " No blame fuss about her."

CHAPTER EIGHT

THE ROUND-UP

THIS, as you well may gather, was in the summer routine. Now the time of the great fall round-up drew near. The home ranch began to bustle in preparation.

All through Cochise County were short mountain ranges set down, apparently at random, like a child's blocks. In and out between them flowed the broad, plain-like valleys. On the valleys were the various ranges, great or small, controlled by the different individuals of the Cattlemen's Association. During the year an unimportant, but certain, shifting of stock took place. A few cattle of Señor Johnson's Lazy Y eluded the vigilance of his riders to drift over through the Grant Pass and into the ranges of his neighbour; equally, many of the neighbour's steers watered daily at Señor Johnson's troughs. It was a matter of courtesy to permit this, but one of the reasons for the fall round-up was a redistribution to the proper ranges. Each cattle-owner sent an outfit to the scene of labour. The combined outfits moved slowly from one valley to another, cutting out the strays, branding the late calves, collecting for the owner of that particular range all his stock, that he might select his marketable beef. In turn each cattleman was host to his neighbours and their men.

This year it had been decided to begin the circle of the round-up at the C O Bar, near the banks of the San Pedro. Thence it would work eastward, wandering slowly in north and south deviation, to include all the country, until the final break-up would occur at the Lazy Y.

The Lazy Y crew was to consist of four men, thirty riding horses, a " chuck wagon," and cook. These, helping others, and receiving help in turn, would suffice, for in the round-up labour was pooled to a common end. With them would ride Jed Parker, to safeguard his master's interests.

For a week the punchers, in their daily rides, gathered in the range ponies. Señor Johnson owned fifty horses which he maintained at the home ranch for every-day riding, two hundred broken saddle animals, allowed the freedom of the range, except when special occasion demanded their use, and perhaps half a thousand quite unbroken—brood mares, stallions, young horses, broncos, and the like. At this time of year it was his habit to corral all those saddlewise in order to select horses for the round-ups and to replace the ranch animals. The latter he turned loose for their turn at the freedom of the range.

The horses chosen, next the men turned their attention to outfit. Each had, of course, his saddle, spurs, and " rope." Of the latter the chuck wagon carried many extra. That vehicle, furthermore, transported such articles as the blankets, the tarpaulins under which to sleep, the running irons for branding, the cooking layout, and the men's personal effects. All was in readiness to move for the six weeks' circle, when a complication arose. Jed Parker, while nimbly escaping an irritated steer, twisted the high heel of his boot on the corral fence. He insisted the injury amounted to nothing. Señor Johnson, however, disagreed.

" It don't amount to nothing, Jed," he pronounced, after manipulation, " but she might make a good able-bodied injury with a little coaxing. Rest her a week and then you'll be all right."

"Rest her, the devil!" growled Jed; "who's going to San Pedro?"

"I will, of course," replied the Señor promptly. "Didje think we'd send the Chink?"

"I was first cousin to a Yaqui jackass for sendin' young Billy Ellis out. He'll be back in a week. He'd do."

"So'd the President," the Señor pointed out; "I hear he's had some experience."

"I hate to have you to go," objected Jed. "There's the missis." He shot a glance sideways at his chief.

"I guess she and I can stand it for a week," scoffed the latter. "Why, we're old married folks by now. Besides, you can take care of her."

"I'll try," said Jed Parker, a little grimly.

CHAPTER NINE

THE LONG TRAIL

The round-up crew started early the next morning, just about sun-up. Señor Johnson rode first, merely to keep out of the dust. Then followed Tom Rich, jogging along easily in the cow-puncher's " Spanish trot," whistling soothingly to quiet the horses, giving a lead to the band of saddle animals strung out loosely behind him. These moved on gracefully and lightly in the manner of the unburdened plains horse, half decided to follow Tom's guidance, half inclined to break to right or left. Homer and Jim Lester flanked them, also riding in a slouch of apparent laziness, but every once in a while darting forward like bullets to turn back into the main herd certain individuals whom the early morning of the unwearied day had inspired to make a dash for liberty. The rear was brought up by Jerky Jones, the fourth cow-puncher, and the four-mule chuck wagon, lost in its own dust.

The sun mounted; the desert went silently through its changes. Wind devils raised straight, true columns of dust six, eight hundred, even a thousand feet into the air. The billows of dust from the horses and men crept and crawled with them like a living creature. Glorious colour, magnificent distance, astonishing illusion, filled the world.

Señor Johnson rode ahead, looking at these things. The separation from his wife, brief as it would be, left room in his soul for the heart-hunger which beauty arouses in men. He loved the charm of the desert, yet it hurt him.

Behind him the punchers relieved the tedium of the march, each after his own manner. In an hour the bunch of loose horses lost its early-morning good spirits and settled down to a steady plodding, that needed no supervision. Tom Rich led them, now, in silence, his time fully occupied in rolling Mexican cigarettes with one hand. The other three dropped back together and exchanged desultory remarks. Occasionally Jim Lester sang. It was always the same song of uncounted verses, but Jim had a strange fashion of singing a single verse at a time. After a long interval he would sing another.

> " My Love is a rider
>   And broncos he breaks,
> But he's given up riding
>   And all for my sake,
> For he found him a horse
>   And it suited him so
> That he vowed he'd ne'er ride
>   Any other bronco ! "

he warbled, and then in the same breath :

" Say, boys, did you get onto the *pisano*-looking shorthorn at Willets last week? "

" Nope."

" He sifted in wearin' one of these hard-boiled hats, and carryin' a brogue thick enough to skate on. Says he wants a job drivin' team—that he drives a truck plenty back to St. Louis, where he comes from. Goodrich sets him behind them little pinto cavallos he has. Say! that son of a gun a driver! He couldn't drive nails in a snow bank." An expressive free-hand gesture told all there was to tell of the runaway. " Th' shorthorn landed headfirst in Goldfish Charlie's horse trough. Charlie fishes him out. ' How the devil, stranger,' says Charlie, ' did you come to fall in here?' ' You blamed fool,' says the shorthorn, just cryin' mad, 'I didn't come to fall in here, I come to drive horses.' "

And then, without a transitory pause:

> "Oh, my Love has a gun
>   And that gun he can use,
> But he's quit his gun fighting
>   As well as his booze.
> And he's sold him his saddle,
>   His spurs, and his rope,
> And there's no more cow-punching
>   And that's what I hope."

The alkali dust, swirled back by a little breeze, billowed up and choked him. Behind, the mules coughed, their coats whitening with the powder. Far ahead in the distance lay the westerly mountains. They looked an hour away, and yet every man and beast in the outfit knew that hour after hour they were doomed, by the enchantment of the land, to plod ahead without apparently getting an inch nearer. The only salvation was to forget the mountains and to fill the present moment full of little things.

But Señor Johnson, to-day, found himself unable to do this. In spite of his best efforts he caught him-

self straining toward the distant goal, becoming
impatient, trying to measure progress by landmarks
—in short acting like a tenderfoot on the desert, who
wears himself down and dies, not from the hardship,
but from the nervous strain which he does not know
how to avoid. Señor Johnson knew this as well as
you and I. He cursed himself vigorously, and began
with great resolution to think of something else.

He was aroused from this by Tom Rich, riding
alongside. " Somebody coming, Señor," said he.

Señor Johnson raised his eyes to the approaching
cloud of dust. Silently the two watched it until it
resolved into a rider loping easily along. In fifteen
minutes he drew rein, his pony dropped immediately
from a gallop to immobility, he swung into a graceful at-ease attitude across his saddle, grinned amiably, and began to roll a cigarette.

" Billy Ellis," cried Rich.

" That's me," replied the newcomer.

" Thought you were down to Tucson? "

" I was."

" Thought you wasn't comin' back for a week
yet? "

" Tommy," proffered Billy Ellis dreamily, " when

you go to Tucson next you watch out until you sees a little, squint-eyed Britisher. Take a look at him. Then come away. He says he don't know nothin' about poker. Mebbe he don't, but he'll outhold a warehouse."

But here Señor Johnson broke in: " Billy, you're just in time. Jed has hurt his foot and can't get on for a week yet. I want you to take charge. I got a lot to do at the ranch."

" Ain't got my war-bag," objected Billy.

" Take my stuff. I'll send yours on when Parker goes."

" All right."

" Well, so long."

" So long, Señor."

They moved. The erratic Arizona breezes twisted the dust of their going. Señor Johnson watched them dwindle. With them seemed to go the joy in the old life. No longer did the long trail possess for him its ancient fascination. He had become a domestic man.

" And I'm glad of it," commented Señor Johnson.

The dust eddied aside. Plainly could be seen the swaying wagon, the loose-riding cowboys, the gleaming, naked backs of the herd. Then the veil closed over them again. But down the wind, faintly, in snatches, came the words of Jim Lester's song:

> " Oh, Sam has a gun
>   That has gone to the bad,
>   Which makes poor old Sammy
>   Feel pretty damn sad,
> For that gun it shoots high,
>   And that gun it shoots low,
> And it wabbles about
>   Like a bucking bronco!"

Señor Johnson turned and struck spurs to his willing pony.

CHAPTER TEN

THE DISCOVERY

Señor Buck Johnson loped quickly back toward the home ranch, his heart glad at this fortunate solution of his annoyance. The home ranch lay in plain sight not ten miles away. As Señor Johnson idly watched it shimmering in the heat, a tiny figure detached itself from the mass and launched itself in his direction.

"Wonder what's eating *him!*" marvelled Señor Johnson, "—and who is it?"

The figure drew steadily nearer. In half an hour it had approached near enough to be recognised.

"Why, it's Jed!" cried the Señor, and spurred his horse. "What do you mean, riding out with that foot?" he demanded sternly, when within hailing distance.

"Foot, hell!" gasped Parker, whirling his horse alongside. "Your wife's run away with Brent Palmer."

For fully ten seconds not the faintest indication proved that the husband had heard, except that he lifted his bridle-hand, and the well-trained pony stopped.

" What did you say? " he asked finally.

" Your wife's run away with Brent Palmer," repeated Jed, almost with impatience.

Again the long pause.

" How do you know? " asked Señor Johnson, then.

" Know, hell! It's been going on for a month. Sang saw them drive off. They took the buckboard. He heard 'em planning it. He was too scairt to tell till they'd gone. I just found it out. They've been gone two hours. Must be going to make the Limited." Parker fidgeted, impatient to be off. " You're wasting time," he snapped at the motionless figure.

Suddenly Johnson's face flamed. He reached from his saddle to clutch Jed's shoulder, nearly pulling the foreman from his pony.

" You lie! " he cried. " You're lying to me! It ain't *so!* "

Parker made no effort to extricate himself from the painful grasp. His cool eyes met the blazing eyes of his chief.

"I wisht I did lie, Buck," he said sadly. "I wisht it wasn't so. But it is."

Johnson's head snapped back to the front with a groan. The pony snorted as the steel bit his flanks, leaped forward, and with head outstretched, nostrils wide, the wicked white of the bronco flickering in the corner of his eye, struck the bee line for the home ranch. Jed followed as fast as he was able.

On his arrival he found his chief raging about the house like a wild beast. Sang trembled from a quick and stormy interrogatory in the kitchen. Chairs had been upset and let lie. Estrella's belongings had been tumbled over. Señor Johnson there found only too sure proof, in the various lacks, of a premeditated and permanent flight. Still he hoped; and as long as he hoped, he doubted, and the demons of doubt tore him to a frenzy. Jed stood near the door, his arms folded, his weight shifted to his sound foot, waiting and wondering what the next move was to be.

Finally, Señor Johnson, struck with a new idea, ran to his desk to rummage in a pigeon-hole. But he found no need to do so, for lying on the desk was what he sought—the check book from which

Estrella was to draw on Goodrich for the money she might need. He fairly snatched it open. Two of the checks had been torn out, stub and all. And then his eye caught a crumpled bit of blue paper under the edge of the desk.

He smoothed it out. The check was made out to bearer and signed Estrella Johnson. It called for fifteen thousand dollars. Across the middle was a great ink blot, reason for its rejection.

At once Señor Johnson became singularly and dangerously cool.

" I reckon you're right, Jed," he cried in his natural voice. " She's gone with him. She's got all her traps with her, and she's drawn on Goodrich for fifteen thousand. And *she* never thought of going just this time of month when the miners are in with their dust, and Goodrich would be sure to have that much. That's friend Palmer. Been going on a month, you say? "

" I couldn't say anything, Buck," said Parker anxiously. " A man's never sure enough about them things till afterwards."

" I know," agreed Buck Johnson; " give me a light for my cigarette."

He puffed for a moment, then rose, stretching his legs. In a moment he returned from the other room, the old shiny Colt's forty-five strapped loosely on his hip. Jed looked him in the face with some anxiety. The foreman was not deceived by the man's easy manner; in fact, he knew it to be symptomatic of one of the dangerous phases of Señor Johnson's character.

" What's up, Buck? " he inquired.

" Just going out for a *pasear* with the little horse, Jed."

" I suppose I better come along? "

" Not with your lame foot, Jed."

The tone of voice was conclusive. Jed cleared his throat.

" She left this for you," said he, proffering an envelope. " Them kind always writes."

" Sure," agreed Señor Johnson, stuffing the letter carelessly into his side pocket. He half drew the Colt's from its holster and slipped it back again. " Makes you feel plumb like a man to have one of these things rubbin' against you again," he observed irrelevantly. Then he went out, leaving the foreman leaning, chair tilted, against the wall.

CHAPTER ELEVEN

THE CAPTURE

ALTHOUGH he had left the room so suddenly, Señor Johnson did not at once open the gate of the adobe wall. His demeanour was gay, for he was a Westerner, but his heart was black. Hardly did he see beyond the convexity of his eyeballs.

The pony, warmed up by its little run, pawed the ground, impatient to be off. It was a fine animal, clean-built, deep-chested, one of the mustang stock descended from the Arabs brought over by Pizarro. Sang watched fearfully from the slant of the kitchen window. Jed Parker, even, listened for the beat of the horse's hoofs.

But Señor Johnson stood stock-still, his brain absolutely numb and empty. His hand brushed against something which fell to the ground. He brought his dull gaze to bear on it. The object proved to be a black, wrinkled spheroid, baked hard as iron in the sun—one of Estrella's toys, a potato squeezed to dryness by the constricting power of the rawhide. In a row along the fence were others. To Señor Johnson it seemed that thus his heart was being squeezed in the fire of suffering.

But the slight movement of the falling object roused him. He swung open the gate. The pony bowed his head delightedly. He was not tired, but his reins depended straight to the ground, and it was a point of honour with him to stand. At the saddle horn, in its sling, hung the riata, the " rope " without which no cowman ever stirs abroad, but which Señor Johnson had rarely used of late. Señor Johnson threw the reins over, seized the pony's mane in his left hand, held the pommel with his right, and so swung easily aboard, the pony's jump helping him to the saddle. Wheel tracks led down the trail. He followed them.

Truth to tell, Señor Johnson had very little idea of what he was going to do. His action was entirely instinctive. The wheel tracks held to the southwest, so he held to the southwest, too.

The pony hit his stride. The miles slipped by. After seven of them the animal slowed to a walk. Señor Johnson allowed him to get his wind, then spurred him on again. He did not even take the ordinary precautions of a pursuer. He did not even glance to the horizon in search.

About supper-time he came to the first ranch house. There he took a bite to eat and exchanged his horse for another, a favourite of his, named Button. The two men asked no questions.

" See Mrs. Johnson go through? " asked the Señor from the saddle.

" Yes, about three o'clock. Brent Palmer driving her. Bound for Willets to visit the preacher's wife, she said. Ought to catch up at the Circle I. That's where they'd all spend the night, of course. So long."

Señor Johnson knew now the couple would follow the straight road. They would fear no pursuit. He himself was supposed not to return for a week, and the story of visiting the minister's wife was not only plausible, it was natural. Jed had upset calculations, because Jed was shrewd, and had eyes in his head. Buck Johnson's first mental numbness was wearing away; he was beginning to think.

The night was very still and very dark, the stars very bright in their candle-like glow. The man, loping steadily on through the darkness, recalled that other night, equally still, equally dark, equally starry, when he had driven out from his accustomed life into the unknown with a woman by his side, the sight of whom asleep had made him feel " almost holy." He uttered a short laugh.

The pony was a good one, well equal to twice the distance he would be called upon to cover this night. Señor Johnson managed him well. By long experience and a natural instinct he knew just how hard to push his mount, just how to keep inside the point where too rapid exhaustion of vitality begins.

Toward the hour of sunrise he drew rein to look about him. The desert, till now wrapped in the thousand little noises that make night silence, drew breath in preparation for the awe of the daily wonder. It lay across the world heavy as a sea of lead, and as lifeless; deeply unconscious, like an exhausted sleeper. The sky bent above, the stars paling. Far away the mountains seemed to wait. And then, imperceptibly, those in the east became blacker and sharper, while those in the west became faintly lucent and lost the distinctness of their outline. The change was nothing, yet everything. And suddenly a desert bird sprang into the air and began to sing.

Señor Johnson caught the wonder of it. The wonder of it seemed to him wasted, useless, cruel in its effect. He sighed impatiently, and drew his hand across his eyes.

The desert became grey with the first light before the glory. In the illusory revealment of it Señor Johnson's sharp frontiersman's eyes made out an object moving away from him in the middle distance. In a moment the object rose for a second against the sky line, then disappeared. He knew it to be the buckboard, and that the vehicle had just plunged into the dry bed of an arroyo.

Immediately life surged through him like an electric shock. He unfastened the riata from its sling, shook loose the noose, and moved forward in the direction in which he had last seen the buckboard.

At the top of the steep little bank he stopped behind the mesquite, straining his eyes; luck had been good to him. The buckboard had pulled up, and Brent Palmer was at the moment beginning a little fire, evidently to make the morning coffee.

Señor Johnson struck spurs to his horse and half slid, half fell, clattering, down the steep clay bank almost on top of the couple below.

Estrella screamed. Brent Palmer jerked out an oath, and reached for his gun. The loop of the riata fell wide over him, immediately to be jerked tight, binding his arms tight to his side.

The bronco-buster, swept from his feet by the pony's rapid turn, nevertheless struggled desperately to wrench himself loose. Button, intelligent at all rope work, walked steadily backward, step by step, taking up the slack, keeping the rope tight as he had done hundreds of times before when a steer had struggled as this man was struggling now. His master leaped from the saddle and ran forward. Button continued to walk slowly back. The riata remained taut. The noose held.

Brent Palmer fought savagely, even then. He kicked, he rolled over and over, he wrenched violently at his pinioned arms, he twisted his powerful young body from Señor Johnson's grasp again and again. But it was no use. In less than a minute he was bound hard and fast. Button promptly slackened the rope. The dust settled. The noise of the combat died. Again could be heard the single desert bird singing against the dawn.

CHAPTER TWELVE

IN THE ARROYO

SENOR JOHNSON quietly approached Estrella. The girl had, during the struggle, gone through an aimless but frantic exhibition of terror. Now she shrank back, her eyes staring wildly, her hands behind her, ready to flop again over the brink of hysteria.

"What are you going to do?" she demanded, her voice unnatural.

She received no reply. The man reached out and took her by the arm.

And then at once, as though the personal contact of the touch had broken through the last crumb of numbness with which shock had overlaid Buck Johnson's passions, the insanity of his rage broke out. He twisted her violently on her face, knelt on her back, and, with the short piece of hard rope the cowboy always carries to "hog-tie" cattle, he lashed her wrists together. Then he arose panting, his square black beard rising and falling with the rise and fall of his great chest.

Estrella had screamed again and again until her face had been fairly ground into the alkali. There she had choked and strangled and gasped and sobbed, her mind nearly unhinged with terror. She kept appealing to him in a hoarse voice, but could get no reply, no indication that he had even heard. This terrified her still more. Brent Palmer cursed steadily and accurately, but the man did not seem to hear him either.

The tempest had broken in Buck Johnson's soul. When he had touched Estrella he had, for the first time, realised what he had lost. It was not the woman—her he despised. But the dreams! All at once he knew what they had been to him—he understood how completely the very substance of his life had changed in response to their slow soul-action. The new world had been blasted—the old no longer existed to which to return.

Buck Johnson stared at this catastrophe until his sight blurred. Why, it was atrocious! He had done nothing to deserve it! Why had they not left him peaceful in his own life of cattle and the trail? He had been happy. His dull eyes fell on the causes of the ruin.

And then, finally, in the understanding of how he had been tricked of his life, his happiness, his right to well-being, the whole force of the man's anger flared. Brent Palmer lay there cursing him artistically. That man had done it; that man was in his power. He would get even. How?

Estrella, too, lay huddled, helpless and defenceless, at his feet. She had done it. He would get even. How?

He had spoken no word. He spoke none now, either in answer to Estrella's appeals, becoming piteous in their craving for relief from suspense, or in response to Brent Palmer's steady stream of insults and vituperations. Such things were far below. The bitterness and anger and desolation were squeezing his heart. He remembered the silly little row of potatoes sewn in the green hide lying along the top of the adobe fence, some fresh and round, some dripping as the rawhide contracted, some black and withered and very small. A fierce and savage light sprang into his eyes.

CHAPTER THIRTEEN

THE RAWHIDE

FIRST of all he unhitched the horses from the buckboard and turned them loose. Then, since he was early trained in Indian warfare, he dragged Palmer to the wagon wheel, and tied him so closely to it that he could not roll over. For, though the broncobuster was already so fettered that his only possible movement was of the jackknife variety, nevertheless he might be able to hitch himself along the ground to a sharp stone, there to saw through the rope about his wrists. Estrella. her husband held in contempt. He merely supplemented her wrist bands by one about the ankles.

Leisurely he mounted Button and turned up the wagon trail, leaving the two. Estrella had exhausted herself. She was capable of nothing more in the way of emotion. Her eyes tight closed, she inhaled in deep, trembling, long-drawn breaths, and exhaled with the name of her Maker.

Brent Palmer, on the contrary, was by no means subdued. He had expected to be shot in cold blood. Now he did not know what to anticipate. His black, level brows drawn straight in defiance, he threw his curses after Johnson's retreating figure.

The latter, however, paid no attention. He had his purposes. Once at the top of the arroyo he took a careful survey of the landscape, now rich with dawn. Each excrescence on the plain his half-squinted eyes noticed, and with instant skill relegated to its proper category of soap-weed, mesquite, cactus. At length he swung Button in an easy lope toward what looked to be a bunch of soap-weed in the middle distance.

But in a moment the cattle could be seen plainly. Button pricked up his ears. He knew cattle. Now he proceeded tentatively, lifting high his little hoofs to avoid the half-seen inequalities of the ground and the ground's growths, wondering whether he were to be called on to rope or to drive. When the rider had approached to within a hundred feet, the cattle started. Immediately Button understood that he was to pursue. No rope swung above his head, so he sheered off and ran as fast as he could to cut ahead of the bunch. But his rider with knee and rein forced him in. After a moment, to his astonishment, he found himself running alongside a big steer. Button had never hunted buffalo—Buck Johnson had.

The Colt's forty-five barked once, and then again. The steer staggered, fell to his knees, recovered, and finally stopped, the blood streaming from his nostrils. In a moment he fell heavily on his side—dead.

Señor Johnson at once dismounted and began methodically to skin the animal. This was not easy, for he had no way of suspending the carcass nor of rolling it from side to side. However, he was practised at it and did a neat job. Two or three times he even caught himself taking extra pains that the thin flesh strips should not adhere to the inside of the pelt. Then he smiled grimly, and ripped it loose.

After the hide had been removed he cut from the edge, around and around, a long, narrow strip. With this he bound the whole into a compact bundle, strapped it on behind his saddle, and remounted. He returned to the arroyo.

Estrella still lay with her eyes closed. Brent

Palmer looked up keenly. The bronco-buster saw the green hide. A puzzled expression crept across his face.

Roughly Johnson loosed his enemy from the wheel and dragged him to the woman. He passed the free end of the riata about them both, tying them close together. The girl continued to moan, out of her wits with terror.

"What are you going to do now, you devil?" demanded Palmer, but received no reply.

Buck Johnson spread out the rawhide. Putting forth his huge strength, he carried to it the pair, bound together like a bale of goods, and laid them on its cool surface. He threw across them the edges, and then deliberately began to wind around and around the huge and unwieldy rawhide package the strip he had cut from the edge of the pelt.

Nor was this altogether easy. At last Brent Palmer understood. He writhed in the struggle of desperation, foaming blasphemies. The uncouth bundle rolled here and there. But inexorably the other, from the advantage of his position, drew the thongs tighter.

And then, all at once, from vituperation the

bronco-buster fell to pleading, not for life, but for death.

"For God's sake, shoot me!" he cried from within the smothering folds of the rawhide. "If you ever had a heart in you, shoot me! Don't leave me here to be crushed in this vise. You wouldn't do that to a yellow dog. An Injin wouldn't do that, Buck. It's a joke, isn't it? Don't go away an' leave me, Buck. I've done you dirt. Cut my heart out, if you want to; I won't say a word, but don't leave me here for the sun——"

His voice was drowned in a piercing scream, as Estrella came to herself and understood. Always the rawhide had possessed for her an occult fascination and repulsion. She had never been able to touch it without a shudder, and yet she had always been drawn to experiment with it. The terror of her doom had now added to it for her all the vague and premonitory terrors which heretofore she had not understood.

The richness of the dawn had flowed to the west. Day was at hand. Breezes had begun to play across the desert; the wind devils to raise their straight columns. A first long shaft of sunlight shot through pass in the Chiricahuas, trembled in the dust-moted air, and laid its warmth on the rawhide. Señor Johnson roused himself from his gloom to speak his first words of the episode.

"There, damn you!" said he. "I guess you'll be close enough together now!"

He turned away to look for his horse.

CHAPTER FOURTEEN

THE DESERT

BUTTON was a trusty of Señor Johnson's private animals. He was never known to leave his master in
the lurch, and so was habitually allowed certain privileges. Now, instead of remaining exactly on the
spot where he was "tied to the ground," he had
wandered out of the dry arroyo bed to the upper
level of the plains, where he knew certain bunch
grasses might be found. Buck Johnson climbed the
steep wooded bank in search of him.

The pony stood not ten feet distant. At his master's abrupt appearance he merely raised his head,
a wisp of grass in the corner of his mouth, without
attempting to move away. Buck Johnson walked
confidently to him, fumbling in his side pocket
for the piece of sugar with which he habitually
soothed Button's sophisticated palate. His hand
ecountered Estrella's letter. He drew it out and
opened it.

"Dear Buck," it read, "I am going away. I tried to be good, but I can't. It's too lonesome for me. I'm afraid of the horses and the cattle and the men and the desert. I hate it all. I tried to make you see how I felt about it, but you couldn't seem to see. I know you'll never forgive me, but I'd go crazy here. I'm almost crazy now. I suppose you think I'm a bad woman, but I am not. You won't believe that. Its' true though. The desert would make anyone bad. I don't see how you stand it. You've been good to me, and I've really tried, but it's no use. The country is awful. I never ought to have come. I'm sorry you are going to think me a bad woman, for I like you and admire you, but nothing, *nothing* could make me stay here any longer." She signed herself simply Estrella Sands, her maiden name.

Buck Johnson stood staring at the paper for a much longer time than was necessary merely to absorb the meaning of the words. His senses, sharpened by the stress of the last sixteen hours, were trying mightily to cut to the mystery of a change going on within himself. The phrases of the letter were bald enough, yet they conveyed something vital to his inner being. He could not understand what it was.

Then abruptly he raised his eyes.

Before him lay the desert, but a desert suddenly and miraculously changed, a desert he had never seen before. Mile after mile it swept away before him, hot, dry, suffocating, lifeless. The sparse vegetation was grey with the alkali dust. The heat hung choking in the air like a curtain. Lizards sprawled in the sun, repulsive. A rattlesnake dragged its loathsome length from under a mesquite. The dried carcass of a steer, whose parchment skin drew tight across its bones, rattled in the breeze. Here and there rock ridges showed with the obscenity of so many skeletons, exposing to the hard, cruel sky the earth's nakedness. Thirst, delirium, death, hovered palpable in the wind; dreadful, unconquerable, ghastly.

The desert showed her teeth and lay in wait like a fierce beast. The little soul of man shrank in terror before it.

Buck Johnson stared, recalling the phrases of the letter, recalling the words of his foreman, Jed Parker. " It's too lonesome for me," " I'm afraid," " I hate it all," " I'd go crazy here," " The desert would make anyone bad," " The country is awful." And the musing voice of the old cattleman, " I wonder if she'll like the country!" They reiterated themselves over and over; and always as refrain his own confident reply, " Like the country? Sure! Why *shouldn't* she? "

And then he recalled the summer just passing, and the woman who had made no fuss. Chance remarks of hers came back to him, remarks whose meaning he had not at the time grasped, but which now he saw were desperate appeals to his understanding. He had known his desert. He had never known hers.

With an exclamation Buck Johnson turned abruptly back to the arroyo. Button followed him, mildly curious, certain that his master's reappearance meant a summons for himself.

Down the miniature cliff the man slid, confidently, without hesitation, sure of himself. His shoulders held squarely, his step elastic, his eye bright, he walked to the fearful, shapeless bundle now lying motionless on the flat surface of the alkali.

Brent Palmer had fallen into a grim silence, but

Estrella still moaned. The cattleman drew his knife and ripped loose the bonds. Immediately the flaps of the wet rawhide fell apart, exposing to the new daylight the two bound together. Buck Johnson leaned over to touch the woman's shoulder.

"Estrella," said he gently.

Her eyes came open with a snap, and stared into his, wild with the surprise of his return.

"Estrella," he repeated, "how old are you?"

She gulped down a sob, unable to comprehend the purport of his question.

"How old are you, Estrella?" he repeated again.

"Twenty-one," she gasped finally.

"Ah!" said he.

He stood for a moment in deep thought, then began methodically, without haste, to cut loose the thongs that bound the two together.

When the man and the woman were quite freed, he stood for a moment, the knife in his hand, looking down on them. Then he swung himself into the saddle and rode away, straight down the narrow arroyo, out beyond its lower widening, into the vast plains the hither side of the Chiricahuas. The alkali dust was snatched by the wind from beneath his horse's feet. Smaller and smaller he dwindled, rising and falling, rising and falling in the monotonous cowpony's lope. The heat shimmer veiled him for a moment, but he reappeared. A mirage concealed him, but he emerged on the other side of it. Then suddenly he was gone. The desert had swallowed him up.

THE END